FORBIDDEN FATES

STOLEN LEGACY, BOOK ONE

CANDICE BUNDY

PIPER FOX

Forbidden Fates
Copyright © 2021
by Candice Bundy and Piper Fox

All rights reserved. No part of this book may be reproduced or transmitted in any form without written permission from the publisher, except by a reviewer who may quote brief passages for review purposes.

This book is a work of fiction and any resemblance to any person, living or dead, any place, events or occurrences, is purely coincidental. The characters and story lines are created from the author's imagination or are used fictitiously.

Identifiers: ISBN-13: 978-1-957446-00-4 (paperback)

Published by Lusios Publishing, Denver, CO.
First Edition, 2021.

CONTENTS

A Simple Favor	1
We're Not in Kansas Anymore	11
Scavenger Hunt	29
More Like a Swap Meet	45
The Runaround	59
Outlaw Rules	69
A Mage on Fire	83
Wait... Fated What's?	103
A Crap Trade	109
Epilogue - Truth and Consequences	121
Also by Candice Bundy	129
Also by Piper Fox	131
About Candice Bundy	133
About Piper Fox	135

A SIMPLE FAVOR
SERA

Despite the pleasant hustle of my day, my magic had been wobbling dangerously out of kilter again. I'd already zapped the shop's La Pavoni barista rig twice, causing it to blow billowing clouds of steam each time. So much for thinking that running a coffee shop slash bookstore slash tabletop gaming destination would be straightforward.

Hah! Gratefully, none of my staff had noticed my magical blips, but why would they? The last thing in the world humans expected was actual magic. It was easier to write me off as a klutz with the equipment than suspect that a supernatural being was hiding out as a glorified barista.

"Critical hit!" came a shout from a room in the back, followed by a chorus of groans. One of our regular teen groups had been reveling in an all-day session, plowing through coffee, muffins, and orcs in equal measure. But by the sound of it, the orcs were gaining an upper hand.

I glanced at the clock. It was just seven p.m., but it felt

later. I was leaving in an hour and couldn't wait for my hot date with an elliptical at the gym. Or perhaps tonight felt more like rowing mojo? No, I needed to burn off this energy before my unstable magic got me in real trouble. Oh, cycling! That was just what I needed to burn down all my excess energy, and I hadn't done that exercise so far this week. The more spazzed out my magic, the harder I needed to work in the gym to burn the edge off.

Then the very last thing I needed walked in through the door of my shop in the form of one Emrys Tedros.

He took a few steps inside, all swagger and momentum, before pausing and looking around. A slight, bemused frown played across his face, like he'd wandered into unknown territory and wasn't sure if he should forge ahead or make a hasty retreat.

He was just as devastatingly handsome as the last time I'd seen him, which was during our days back at Goldenbriar Academy over four years ago. He'd cut his dark, curly hair short since, which I imagined had broken a few hearts. Emrys scrubbed a hand down the perfectly groomed stubble along his jawline for a moment before his gaze caught mine. His lips curled as he looked me over, and I hated the flush of heat that rolled over me in response. Crap, did I just blush?

Emrys showing up in my shop, of all places, couldn't be a simple coincidence. He definitely wasn't here for the nerdy goodness of gaming or a caramel latte that he certainly could have gotten much closer to home. He must have come looking for me, but why?

Never mind the why. Emrys showing up meant trouble.

Pepper, my evening barista and shop tender, sidled up next to me as she wiped the workspace clean. "Wowie, that smooth player belongs in a nightclub, not a coffee shop filled with geeky gamers. You think he fell in here by accident?"

Pepper had worked for me for the past two years, and I never had to worry about where I stood with her. She was as solid and reliable as she was outspoken, despite me being her boss. Pepper was right though. Emrys was dressed in black pants and a button-down shirt which all looked tailored and expensive. He would have fit in better at a wine bar or posh club downtown.

"Emrys doesn't end up anywhere by accident," I muttered.

She turned to me, doing a double take. "Oh, you're on a first-name basis with Emrys, is it? Aren't you full of surprises with your supermodel friends? If he's your new thing, let me just say, yum-my," she replied, breaking the last word into two syllables.

I shook my head at her. "He's neither my new thing nor my old thing." Although there had been moments at academy when, based on his interest, it could have been more, but I'd always kept a careful distance.

Yeah, Emrys was definitely a... something. Sure, he was crazy hot, even without that luscious long dark hair, often acting like he was a gift from the gods to all women. Then again, he was straight up a demigod, so maybe he had it half right. Emrys hailed from the goddess Isis' lineage, his beauty and charisma turning heads wherever he went. Pepper's reaction didn't surprise me, but I couldn't forget how tiresome his overconfidence in his own prowess could be.

I also couldn't forget that I owed him a favor.

"The way he's looking at you, you might need to

explain that to him. Here comes mister smoldering eyes now," Pepper whispered. "I know when to bow out." She turned tail and headed around the counter, no doubt intent on busy work that would keep her within earshot.

Emrys walked up to the counter, his eyes drinking me in as he approached. I was suddenly very much aware of the coffee and chocolate sauce stains on my apron. Also, that I was wearing an apron. Not that Emrys seemed to notice any of that.

What if, instead of hitting the gym, I spent a quality hour or two with him? I let the idea roll around in my brain for a few seconds, relishing in the dopamine hit, before I dismissed the thought as foolhardy. I avoided the supernatural community for a reason, and the last thing I needed was a demigod hanging around. Although, from what I'd heard, Emrys was not the type to stick around.

When he stopped at the counter, I waited a moment for him to speak. He seemed lost, almost as if I'd enchanted him, which was so totally not even within the realm of possibility with my messed-up magic. What was up with him? He seemed almost nervous, but surely that couldn't be right.

I leaned against the counter. "What brings you to my Charmed Brews, Emrys?"

He hitched that persuasive smile of his. "This is quite the little establishment, Seraphina. Not at all what I'd expected."

Not at all actually magical, must be what he was thinking. "You didn't answer my question."

"Do you have a few minutes to talk?" He arched his brow. "Privately?"

I pursed my lips. Did I want to know? "Maybe. Maybe

not," I answered, hearing the lie on my lips. A thrill of excitement ran through me. Of course I wanted to know why Emrys was here. "Did you come all this way for a caramel latte?"

His eyes sparkled with anticipation. "You know how to tempt me, but I fear I'm short on time."

"No time for a latte?"

"Afraid not. Can we please talk?" he pressed. "It's an urgent matter."

Please? Okay, now my curiosity was locked and loaded. I cast my gaze around the store. Everyone appeared caught up in their own little worlds, and Pepper could handle things for a bit.

"Come around the counter, there's a space we can use in the back," I replied, and then turned to Pepper. "Can you take over for a few minutes?"

She shot me a sly smile. "Sure thing, boss."

Emrys followed me through a door at the end of the counter, down a short hall, and into a room we used as a pantry. When we got there, I turned to face him.

"What's all this about?"

Emrys didn't speak, and again I had the sense he was feeling hesitant, which was so out of character. I didn't know what to make of it.

"Out with it, Emrys. Why are you here?"

"I'm in a bit of a pinch," he said, a frown creasing his brow. "And I was hoping you could help me out?"

What in the world could he need me for? I couldn't deny being intrigued, but I had to tease him back. "The brash Emrys is in trouble. How am I not surprised?" I asked, to which he held up his hand to his mouth, pretending shock. I shook my head. "What have you got yourself into this time?"

"The boys and I—" he began, but I cut him off.

"The boys?" I barked out a laugh. "You're still hanging with your posse from our academy days?"

He frowned, but the humor from before had vanished. "Ours is a true brotherhood, Sera. While we don't see each other frequently, our bond remains deep."

"Yeah, okay. So what trouble did you and 'the boys' get yourselves into this time?"

He glanced around us, as if checking to make sure we were alone, which was silly, because we were behind a shut door. "Tink is messing with us. She took some items from us and is holding them hostage. I'm hoping you can talk some sense into her."

I sighed. "By 'Tink,' I assume you mean our fae alumna from Goldenbriar, Taneisha?" He gave me a single grave nod. I shook my head, sighing again. Their petty rivalry had been nonstop during academy, kept in line as far as I could tell, only by fear of expulsion. "I would have thought you'd learned to leave her, and really any fae, alone by now?"

Emrys lifted his hands up defensively. "I swear we didn't start it this time. None of us have even seen or talked with her since our academy days."

"You may think that, but we know the fae never drop grudges, Em," I replied. His lip curled at my use of his nickname.

He leaned close, placing his hand over mine. A slight electric charge traveled between us. When Emrys spoke, it was in a low, hushed tone. I felt the timbre in his voice like a wave of heat rolling over my skin. "You always got along with her, Sera. Plus, you have an uncanny ability to persuade people to your way of thinking. Would you be willing to have a word with Tink on our behalf? I bet you could talk some sense into her, if anyone can."

There it was. The ask. I shook my head. "No one can talk a fae out of a grudge."

He flashed me that sultry smile of his again, and then he chuckled. "The Seraphina Lowe I remember could talk a selkie out of their pelt. Besides, Tink likes you."

I felt my cheeks flush at his compliment. Yet Emrys didn't know what he was asking. I'd lived apart, hiding myself and my faulty magic, for years. I hadn't even finished Goldenbriar in person, partly out of fear I'd harm others with my wayward magic. The other part was all about salvaging my family's spotless reputation as some of the most powerful mages around.

Except me. My magic was potent, sure, but also unreliable and difficult to control, even on the best of days.

"Look, just have one conversation with Ti... I mean Taneisha," he said. "Get her to see reason and drop this thing with us. I swear we'll never even talk to her again if we can get this cleared up."

I hated to admit it, but I was enjoying being around the demigod, even when I knew he was a bit of a scoundrel. I missed my academy days. I even missed Em's "boys." Cadre? Posse? Whatever.

Maybe, if I hadn't been living off the supernatural grid, his offer wouldn't have been so compelling. Yet I was, and it was.

I couldn't deny craving everything Em was offering. A little adventure. A bit of a challenge. A brief visit with the magical community I missed. Reminiscing with friends from the academy. Seeing his posse, and even Taneisha, could be fun––an adventure even. A welcome break from the relative humdrum of my normal, magic-free life.

What would be the harm? My family would never have to know, and it's not like I'd have to use my magic to talk to Taneisha.

I let myself hold on to that thought for a moment. Then another.

"Sorry, Emrys. I can't." If my family found out I was risking exposing our spotless reputation as the most esteemed and powerful mages around, I'd have hell to pay.

Emrys took a step back as if I'd hit him. I could practically hear the gears spinning in his head. His expression turned pained, but then he flashed another of his gorgeous smiles. I could almost feel the proverbial Damocles' sword hanging in the air.

He stepped close, leaning against the pantry shelving behind me, effectively boxing me in. This close, I could feel the heat of his body, even though he wasn't touching me. My mind clouded, overrun with unbidden images. What would his stubble feel like against my neck? Or his hands against the small of my back, or gripping my hips?

"I don't want to strong-arm you, Sera, but I'm really in a bind. I have to call in the favor owed."

Emrys' words brought me out of my reverie. "What, for a simple conversation? You'd waste a favor in return for a chat?"

He shrugged. "I'm low on options and even shorter on time. All I'm asking for is you to spend a short while talking with her, using your influence on my brotherhood's behalf."

I ground my teeth. If I refused a favor owed, Emrys had

every right to spread the word in the supe community that my word meant nothing. Personally, I couldn't care, as I lived apart, but the damage to my reputation would tarnish my family as well.

"Alright, Em. I'll talk to Taneisha for you." I held up a finger in warning. "But no guarantees, and you all will owe me a favor each in return for helping, even if I can't change her mind."

He arched his brow. "You're not allowed to demand reciprocal favors. That's against the rules of polite society."

I arched a brow right back at him. "Can't I? First, I only owe you a favor, not the others. Second, this is a last-minute emergency I have to drop everything for." Which wasn't anything besides my date with the elliptical, but he didn't need to know that. My time mattered, even if it wasn't magic-related. "And third, it's pretty clear you want this business kept quiet."

He spread his hands wide, and his smile melted the last trickle of resistance within me. "Fair enough. That's all I can ask." Emrys took my hand in his and headed for the door. "Let's go."

"Wait. Now?"

"Yes. No time like the present, right?"

I pulled away. "Let me grab my purse." I ran back to the front, taking off my apron as I went.

Pepper looked up at my return, giving me the once-over. Was she checking to see if my clothes were out of place? I almost laughed.

"Are you taking off early?" Pepper asked, a knowing smile on her face.

"Yeah." I felt a little embarrassed. But why should I?

Besides, it wasn't what Pepper thought. Even if it was, so what? "Can you watch the store until I get back?"

"Will do. I'm opening tomorrow already too, in case you feel the need to sleep in," she said, and then winked at me.

I rolled my eyes. "I trust you to hold down the fort while I'm gone. Thanks, Pepper, you're fantastic."

Emrys whisked me out the door, my heart beating fast and my magic percolating at a low simmer.

Hopefully, Taneisha would be in a reasonable mood. If not, at least I'd have some favors owed to me, and I could leave the boys and the fae to work out their differences.

WE'RE NOT IN KANSAS ANYMORE

SERA

I luxuriated in the feel of the wind whipping through my hair as Emrys sped us through the city streets in his black convertible Porsche sports car. Compared to my practical and rugged SUV, it was an excess I would never have imagined buying, even if I had the funds. But it fit Emrys and his playboy reputation perfectly.

"What's that on your shirt?" he asked.

I looked down at the D-20 die embossed on my black t-shirt with the '20' in glittery gold letters. "It's a nat twenty."

Emrys tilted his head to the side. "A what?"

"It's an automatic hit," I explained. He shook his head. Of course he didn't get gamer lingo. "It's gaming lingo for an automatic win."

"Oh, well," he said, smiling like he understood that much, "of course you are."

I shook my head. His confidence could float an iron brick. I always used to enjoy Emrys' banter and flirtation, and we'd done a fair amount during my short stint at the academy, but today, it grated on my nerves.

"What was that place?"

"It's my business," I replied, feeling a bit of pride. "It stays pretty hopping, even until the wee hours. We've got tabletop gamers who book out the rooms in the back, the coffee shop up front, and books and games we sell."

He frowned. "So is this establishment like a deep cover for the magic contracts you do?"

I answered with a non-answer. "What do you think?"

"I think it's clever. You're accessible, and if any mundane hears you talking about spells, gods, or enchantments, they'll assume it's gaming related."

I smirked, but looked away, unable to face the look of admiration on his face for credit I did not earn. "Something like that."

"I'm not surprised. Your family has always been so secretive about the work you do, and yet, most everyone I know has contracted with them at one point or another. It's like they've got their hands in everything."

I nodded but didn't confirm or deny his string of assumptions. I might not be in on the family business, but I knew the art of being cagey to a T.

By the time we reached our destination, screeching to a stop in a well-lit parking lot, I'd half-forgotten why I was even with him. He was such a showoff. "Thanks, Emrys."

"Please, Sera, call me Em like you used to."

I arched my brow and shot him my 'quit your bullshit' look, and his smug smile faltered.

"Where are we now?"

Emrys pointed up at a sign. "Franc's club."

The word Velvet glowed overhead, not so subtly

beckoning us into what I could only assume was a den of iniquity suitable for the hedonistic god of decadence. "So we are."

Em jumped out of the car, ran around, opened my door, and offered me his hand. I took it, grateful for the haul up from the car's ground-level bucket seats. The momentum brought us face to face, our bodies brushing against each other. I let out a little gasp, to which Em hitched a smile.

"The guys are waiting for us inside," he said, his voice a low rumble.

I took a step back, pulling my hand from his, but it didn't dispel the tension between us. Velvet was only ten minutes from my coffee shop, but it was another world away with the supe community. "Of course they are."

"Haven't you been to Franc's club before?" he asked.

Like Emrys, Franc was also a demigod, except he hailed from Dionysos. As the only two demigods in our class, of course they'd become fast friends. I'd heard Franc had a nightclub. I mean, what else did you expect from a demigod of drunkenness and ecstasy?

"I haven't." It might have been physically close, but it was far away from my supe comfort zone. I imagined all of Emrys' cadre waiting for us beyond those tall, imposing doors, and a shiver of anticipation ran down my spine. "It doesn't look open."

"Velvet is always open, at least to me," Emrys replied with a wink, leading me into the belly of the beast.

The balls on this guy. I chuckled to myself as we walked in the door. The atmosphere of the club hit me all at once. The under-lit mood lighting in shades of rose and red, seemingly everywhere, made me feel like we were entering an underworld secret society. The music, with a low, thrumming beat, made my hips sway with every step I took. There was even the scent of whiskey and cigars lingering in the air, as well as a hint of animalistic musk.

It felt like I'd definitely entered the belly of the beast, and my negotiations with the troublesome fae hadn't even started. At the reminder, I felt instantly keyed up over the prospect of seeing the boys again. For the short time I'd known them at school, they'd all made lasting impressions on me.

Then we turned a corner, and I stopped short as we came face to face with the others. The guys were gathered around a high-top table at the side of a dance floor, no longer the youths I'd gone to school with. No, they were all men now, with even broader shoulders, more facial hair, and somehow, impossibly, even more swagger.

I wouldn't be surprised if that scent of musk in the air was all them. Goddess, help me. I was looking for a brief adventure, wasn't I? I hadn't expected to fall into a class 10 thirst trap.

Almost in unison, their gazes all affixed on me. I shifted on my feet and raised my chin, feeling the sudden need to square off against their raw intensity. By the surprised looks on their faces, and a couple of frowns, I wasn't what they'd expected or hoped for. Or perhaps they hadn't thought Emrys could persuade me to help?

"What was that? We're in a trap?" Liam asked, his intense emerald-eyed gaze boring into me.

I'd said that out loud? I felt my cheeks heat. Maybe I'd muttered and his shifter ears had picked it up?

"Oh nothing, I was just thinking about work."

Argh, I wanted to slap myself in the forehead. I was grateful when the conversation moved on.

"About time you got back," Franc said, walking over to us. He was an imposing figure. Lean and tall with sky-blue eyes, blond hair, and clean shaven, he'd always reminded me of a Viking warrior, despite his Dionysian lineage. "We thought you wouldn't make it," he said to Emrys, his voice terse.

Emrys checked his watch and then shrugged. "We're here in time. Besides, Sera and I had to catch up a little. As you can see, she came along and has offered to reason with Tink on our behalf."

Franc tilted his head to the side and looked me over. "It might help. Thanks for coming along."

"You're welcome," I replied.

Liam, a wolf shifter, and Marcos, a panther shifter, shared a look, and then both frowned deeper. I remembered their habit of silent communication, something innate to shifters, and wondered what they weren't saying aloud.

Caden, an incubus, gestured toward me, shaking his head. "She's your big solution?" he said to Emrys, but then looked at me. "No offense or anything, Sera, but Em shouldn't have involved you."

Despite Caden's tone, I couldn't help the tingle of pleasure that washed over me when he spoke. I glanced at his neck, seeing the silvered chain that hung there and relaxed. I remembered him wearing it at the academy, the item specially made for the incubi who attended, so their powers wouldn't overrun the entire student body. I appreciated Caden still had his powers on a short leash.

Otherwise, the others and I would have had to summon monumental willpower to withstand his draw.

Willpower wasn't something I was overflowing with at the moment.

"I have my reasons," Emrys replied under his breath.

Based on the unusual tension between the men, whatever Taneisha was up to, it must have been more serious than Emrys had let on. I could have taken it as a warning, but it only piqued my curiosity. Just how much trouble did she have them in?

"None taken," I replied. "If you don't want my help, I'll go, but I got to know Taneisha fairly well during our academy days. If there's room to negotiate, I'll find it."

They all shared a troubled look.

"Em explained the situation to you?" Franc asked, holding up an oblong, carved rock in his hand about the size of a dinner plate. There were symbols on it which glowed in the dim light, and I recognized one as a fae sigil.

"At a high level," Emrys said.

The men all turned to him. Based on their concerned expressions, I could guess Em had left out some key details of their troubles with the fae. Was what I was getting myself into worse than having my reputation damaged from not honoring the favor owed?

The stone chimed, and then the glowing of the symbols intensified. Franc held it out to the others, who gathered around and, one by one, placed their hands on the stone. First Caden, and then Marcos. With each added contact, the symbols flared with brighter light.

"We're out of time and out of options," Liam said, placing his hand on the rock. "Thanks, Sera, but you should go home. We'll have to figure things out on our own."

The stone emitted a second, louder chime, which echoed through the cavernous club.

"Now, Em," Franc ordered. "The third chime could happen at any moment."

In a final gesture of invitation, Em reached out for my hand, inviting me along one last time. Watching them all standing side by side, headed off to adventure together, was an intoxication I hadn't realized existed. All I wanted to do was join the cadre, just this once, and relive some of my youth.

When I took his hand, I felt a smile spread across my face. Standing between Em and Marcos, I placed my hand on the stone between theirs. My excitement stood in contrast to the men, who ranged from Franc and Em's tense, to Caden's sullen, to Liam's grouchy, to Marcos' resigned determination.

Before I could debate my admittedly questionable motivations for joining them, the third chime hit with the force of a gong clanging against my head. From the sudden, pained expressions on the others' faces, they'd shared the same experience. A whirlwind formed, encasing the six of us in a dark, spinning globe. It sucked all the air out of my lungs as the wind rushed around us.

Just when my lungs strained, a wave of energy burst from the stone, slamming into me and throwing me to the ground. The next instant the gust died down, and we were somewhere else altogether.

Somewhere fantastical.

My head was spinning, but I sat up, rubbing my temples. The still-glowing stone sat on the ground between us. The magic portal had knocked all of us down to the ground. I got my bearings and waited for the dizziness to pass, taking slow, even breaths. As my heart rate and breathing leveled out, I took in our new surroundings.

We were now in a forest glen, reminiscent of children's storybook perfection. Surrounded by towering aspen and pine trees, the carpeted vale had a small pond alongside, with the babbling sound of water flowing into it. An ornately carved and framed door stood at the far end of the grove, the one item that hadn't sprung forth directly from nature itself. Colorful wildflowers dotted the surrounding space, and I assumed they were the source of the abundant floral scent invading my nose.

The very air reeked of magic. I could feel the magic flow through my veins, responding to some unspoken call. I felt downright fuzzy, both emotionally and physically. Somehow, I could sense the texture of the moss and the taste of the water. I could almost make out a message in the rustling of the aspen leaves in the breeze. Even the sounds of the men breathing, swallowing, and moving around had turned up to eleven.

Okay, this had never happened before. I'd never been through a fae portal, although I'd learned about them at school. Despite feeling uncomfortably hypersensitive here, Faery was an amazing, if weird place.

One thing was for sure. Already this brief adventure was paying off so far in new experiences. I was reserving judgment for whether I'd later classify these as fun.

Emrys stood and then offered me his hand. He hauled me up for the second time tonight. My balance wasn't quite a hundred percent yet, so I leaned against him for a moment, watching the others stand up and get their bearings.

"This place is amazing. We must be in some sort of fae dimension," I said, scratching a sudden itch running along my right shoulder blade.

Caden rolled his eyes at me. "Do you have more of that boundless fae 101 material to bless us with on our quest?" I could hear the irritation in his tone, but I also felt an undercurrent of worry off him.

I pulled away from Emrys. The awareness of others' emotions was new to me. I liked to think I read people fairly well, but I wasn't an empath. Could it be the fae magic of this place?

Liam growled at him, and I could practically hear his wolf just underneath the surface, poised to defend me. But why? "That's uncalled for. Sera's just remarking on how odd this place is, and she's right. Have you been to Faery before?"

Caden shrugged. "Why would I want to? This place looks boring and there aren't enough women."

"Who says you need women to have fun?" Franc said, hinting at a history that was certainly new territory since I'd known them last. He breathed deep, seeming to luxuriate in the energy of this place. "I like it here. It's got fun vibes."

"You would," Emrys replied, shaking his head. He looked around the circle. "Does anyone else feel odd?"

"I do," I replied, scratching the left side of my neck where it met my shoulder. "Kind of dizzy? Woozy? Hypersensitive."

The others nodded agreement, and right away the tension was back. And what was up with my skin? Was I allergic to fae forests? Hiving from an overdose of testosterone?

"I feel super aware. Like I can sense your feelings," Emrys said. A giggle escaped me. "You're enjoying this?" he asked me.

"Yeah, why not?"

"Things don't feel different to me," Macros added. "I'm used to sensing other shifters' emotions, so it's not really an unfamiliar experience. Just new with all of you."

Liam gave a nod of agreement. "Same." He turned to me, his attention drawn to my scratching. He dipped his chin, eyes turning predatory. "Are you okay?"

That look, wowza. If he was going to play the big bad wolf, I wouldn't mind being devoured. Which would be a bad idea, but a gal could dream, right?

I looked away, shaking my head. "Yeah. Sure. It's nothing." Maybe it was just my nerves? "Maybe it's magic designed to put us off our game?"

The men shared glances. Franc and Emrys both nodded. Caden was staring off into space at the water. Liam and Marcos did that shifter-mind-meld thing again.

"I don't trust it. Hopefully, the flighty fae will be reasonable," Emrys said.

"Maybe the emotional bleed is because of the stone?" Marcos asked, but it was a rhetorical question. I had the impression his panther was itching to pace out his tension, but Marcos' feet remained firmly planted right where he stood.

"We'll have to ask Tink," Franc replied.

"You'd do well to call her Taneisha," I said.

"You always were the clever one," came a familiar voice from behind me. I turned to face Taneisha, who'd appeared behind me. She was practically glowing in a golden gown that fit her like a glove, with blue butterfly wings covering it. No, scratch that. The dress was glowing, and the butterflies were living blue morphos.

Nice to know Taneisha hadn't lost her flair for the dramatic.

"Seraphina Lowe. You? Here? Now? Color me surprised!"

"Well, I get out. Rarely, but it happens. How've you been?"

Taneisha let out a melodious laugh. "Never better." She clapped her hands, and the glowing stone disappeared in a puff of yellow and black swallowtail butterflies. Was I sensing a theme? "We won't be needing that anymore."

"This place is amazing. Is it a pocket universe?" I asked her.

Taneisha pursed her lips, and the barest of frowns creasing her brows. "You're not familiar?" She narrowed her perceptive gaze on me as she sauntered closer.

I had to be careful. She couldn't learn about my screwy magic.

"I keep plenty busy, but portals and fae magic are not within my area of expertise."

There was the barest pause before Taneisha's smile widened again. "Pshaw. Why would they be for a mage of your standing? Now, I know why the boys answered my summons, willingly coming into my dominion. I took their precious trinkets and threatened to destroy the items unless they arrived here at the appointed time. That's how blackmail works."

I wanted to ask what Taneisha had taken. Whatever it

was, it was enough to drag all the posse here, submitting to her will.

"An age-old motivation, to be sure," I replied.

Taneisha leaned in closer, eyes lit with curiosity, and spoke in low tones. "But tell me, Sera. What brought you here?"

I debated playing coy, but who was I kidding? It's not like I could out-trick a fae. Ballsy and direct were my best bets. For the briefest of moments, I debated telling her I came along for the adventure alone or simply confessing the mediocrity of my day-to-day life. But Emrys had called in his favor, and it was incumbent on me to at least try to get the boys' items back from Taneisha.

"Emrys asked me to act as mediator, hoping to resolve this situation. I understand there's an old grudge in play. I remember enough of our years at the academy together to know they no doubt earned every ounce of your ill will." I glanced back at the five men, who were wisely keeping their mouths shut. "They assured me they're repentant," at least they look like it now, "and will swear vows to avoid you and your dominion. Name a price for them to pay, and you'll never have to deal with them, or their poor behavior, again."

Yeah, I was taking some liberties here, but I hadn't exactly received a detailed brief to strategize from. It wasn't the first time I'd run a campaign with less than thirty minutes' notice. This wasn't a game, yet strategy was strategy. It would have to be good enough.

"That's fine, Sera, but we're a little beyond the 'let's shake hands and move on' stage now."

I held up my hands. "I don't see why we have to be? I'm sure the boys, I mean the men, can provide reparations much more suited to your needs than whatever trinkets you took from them."

"I'm listening to you fairly because I always liked you, Sera. You make a fair argument. Understand, their trinkets hold no value for me. I have no need of earthly wealth. Years ago, I vowed these boys would pay when the time was right. The vow cannot be undone, and their time is now. I reject your offer."

My shoulders slumped. "I understand. Thanks for hearing me out." I turned to Emrys. "Sorry, I tried." He nodded, a grave expression on his face. "Can you use that door to send me back home?" I asked Taneisha.

She crossed her arms, lips pouting in disappointment. "I guess you're not the clever one after all, even though you finished at the top of our class. Did you not pay attention in Fae Portals 101?"

A nagging anxiety crawled over my skin. There was no such class, but the fae loved to speak in metaphor. I couldn't help it. My gaze flicked to Caden, who was running a hand through his chin-length black hair. Then he looked up at me, his raised brows seeming to ask, "Well, did you?"

Hmm, maybe? I scratched at the hives on my right shoulder again.

"Hey!" Taneisha snapped her fingers in front of me, drawing my attention back to her. "I was talking. What's wrong with you?"

I turned my shoulder toward her, pulling my v-neck t-shirt collar to the side for her to see. "It's some sort of allergy or hive thing," I said. "It itches, a lot!"

Taneisha's face scrunched with momentary confusion. "Curious."

I forced myself to stop scratching. "It's not important."

"Alright," she replied, intoning the word, but then her face perked up, utterly filled with cheer. "I'm unhappy Emrys and the others dragged you into this, Sera, but then, here you are. We must trust fate with these matters. Right?"

I didn't want reassurances in fate from Taneisha, or anyone else. Fate had been perfectly clear that my life, and my magic, were of no concern to anyone. For the sake of negotiations, I held my tongue.

"As I was saying, by coming through the portal with them, you answered and accepted my summons, joining your fate with theirs. There's nothing to be done about it now but to soldier forward."

I fisted my hands and crossed my arms, holding my midsection tight. She couldn't be serious! Why would she even want me here? "That's not true. This is your summons. Your pocket universe. Your rules. You're all powerful here, Taneisha. You can change whatever you like. Please send me home."

Taneisha shrugged. "I'm glad to hear you have a full grasp of the situation. You picked your side, Sera. I hope it works out for you."

I blinked slowly as I processed her words, realizing that the mercurial fae had no intention of letting me go. Whatever plans she had for the boys, I was along for the ride. However long that lasted.

Could anyone blame me for launching myself at her? A sparkle lit Taneisha's eyes, and she raised her hands, a swirl of gray mist forming between them.

I didn't get far. Just two steps toward her and firm yet gentle hands came around my midsection, lifted me up, and gracefully moved me back to where the boys were gathered, despite my protests.

"You're okay," Marcos whispered in my ear. His steady presence cooled the burn of my anger. Despite myself, I struggled against him. "I'd love to watch you take her down, but you can't win against a fae in their realm. Just breathe."

I hated it, but he was right. I could never best a fae within her magical home base. I also couldn't muster enough magic, or control it long enough, to blast her socks off. But none of them needed to know that.

"What kind of mage are you, that you resort to blows?" Franc asked.

I glowered at Franc but didn't answer. Marcos ran his hand down my arm, a simple, yet both supportive and calming gesture, and I relaxed against him.

"A fair question, wine-borne, but it'll have to wait," Taneisha replied, allowing the mist between her hands to dissipate. "Enough distractions. It's high time I outlined the rules of this game. I have your priceless heirlooms, and it's on you to win them back, if you can." Her smug smile implied this would be no small feat.

I looked Marcos, who still had a protective arm around me, in the eye. He looked me over, and for a moment I felt so safe. I didn't want to go anywhere else. When I gave a slight shrug, he let go, but he didn't move away.

A fire in his eyes, Emrys stepped forward. "You had no right to steal our legacies from us."

Taneisha turned to him. "And you had no right to be so cruel to me, and yet you were. It's not my fault you brought all your priceless trinkets to Velvet and then partied so hard you didn't even notice me taking them. Perhaps you would have been wise to lock them up."

"I told you so," Caden murmured under his breath, but I think we all heard it.

"Your legacies, as you call them, will remain mine unless you can win them back. You'll have a single opportunity to regain each item. If you fail, it will be lost to you forever."

"What will you do with our legacies if we fail?" Liam asked.

"Burn them. Shatter them. Crush them. Emulsify them with a nice avocado oil and feed them to my pets. What does it matter? They'll be gone, and you will each pay a hefty price for your folly."

Once again, the air was thick with tension. The boys didn't argue with her or plead. Did they fear Taneisha would destroy their objects if they argued?

What were these precious items, anyway?

Taneisha flicked her wrist toward the doorway and it swung open, revealing a city street I didn't recognize. People were bustling about, paying no mind to the open door into Faery before them.

"You have until noon tomorrow to find Marcos' legacy," she said. "That's just over twenty-four hours from when I'm re-inserting you."

I looked up at him, but his focus was single-mindedly on Taneisha.

"How do I find it?" Marcos asked.

"Since it's the first trial, and you were the least terrible to me, Marcos, I'm making it easy for you. You get a scavenger hunt. Go through the door, find the Eye of the Tiger, and bring it to me."

Marcos placed his right hands on his hip. "Just one item?"

"Yes."

Caden let out a derisive snicker. "You can't call one item a scavenger hunt."

"Oh, can't I?" She rolled her eyes at him. "I'm sure I can call it whatever I want."

"How do we find you?" Emrys asked.

"That's easy. Get into a secluded location and say my name three times in a row. Oh, I almost forgot. Don't play this fast and loose and try to cheat your way out of this. You must negotiate in good faith to get the Eye. No cheating. No stealing. If you break the rules, there will be consequences." She turned her narrowed gaze at each of them, as if daring them to further challenge her. "Now get a move on. Your countdown is already running out, boys. Or folks, I suppose, now that you have a plus-one." Taneisha said and then winked at me.

SCAVENGER HUNT
MARCOS

The door to Faery slammed shut behind us with an air of finality. The frame on this side was the front door to a nondescript shoe repair store. I was confident the link to Taneisha's faery realm had severed the moment it closed.

Taneisha had us by the tails, including Seraphina, who didn't at all deserve to be here. I expected she could handle whatever Taneisha threw at us, but it was time away from her life and responsibilities she hadn't counted on. I'd have to pin Em down later and find out what hell he was thinking by dragging her along.

Not that I minded being around Sera. If anything, I was having a tough time keeping my eyes off the geeky mage. Watching Sera take on Taneisha on our behalf flipped some sort of switch in my head. I couldn't remember the last time anyone had worked to defend me, much less someone with such a glorious, curvaceous ass or such a cute pixie nose.

I shook my head. I needed to keep my head in the

game, not getting soft on a standoffish, brainy mage from my academy days, no matter how cute she was.

"That could have gone better," Franc said, scrubbing a hand through his hair. "What godsforsaken place are we at now? And when?"

"I bet Marcos knows where we are," Sera said. "It's his legacy item quest, after all. As for when? Based on the angle of the sun, it's midmorning. Were we in Faery that long?"

My name on Sera's lips sent a thrill down my spine, and my panther purred in response. Well, that was different.

"Time runs differently there," Emrys replied. "Hopefully we only lost one evening."

I glanced up and down the street, which I'd assumed was the main drag of this small town. Aware of everyone's gaze on me, I sniffed the air. Bittersweet images of digging into blackberry pies, getting my fur matted with mud while wrestling with other young shifters after a spring rain, and the scent of my mother's shampoo washed over me. It was all too familiar, even if it had been nearly a decade ago.

"Yeah, I know this place. It's my aunt's village, Golden," I replied.

I hadn't been back here since my dad left town with me when I was thirteen. Would anyone even recognize me after all this time?

"So then, we're certain this is the real world?" Emrys asked. "Not just some fae imagining?"

"Most likely," I said. "Unless it's a false reality Taneisha spun up just to mess with us."

"But why would that matter?" Liam asked, his voice a

low rumble. "Whether real or some alternate faery realm, we still have to play the fae's games to get our legacies back."

"If it's real, we should send Sera home," Emrys replied. "There's no reason for you to stay," he said to her, his concern appearing genuine. "I'm sorry I dragged you into this, Sera. You should go home and leave us to the fae's games."

"Let's assume this is real," I said. "We're in Canada now. A small town of a few thousand in British Columbia. We'd have to drive a couple hours to put her on a plane."

Even as I said the words, the idea of sending Sera off, of watching her leave, didn't sit well with me or my panther. I wanted her where I could see her. Keep track of her scent.

Shaking her head, Sera crossed her arms. "You don't have time for that. Besides, I have to stay with you. Taneisha declared it. I will not be the reason you lose your precious whatsits. You can all just owe me another favor."

It was shrewd thinking on Seraphina's part. I couldn't fault her for charging us for her time either.

"What favors would a mage need from us?" Caden asked, digging his hands into the front pocket of his black jeans as he leaned against the wall of the repair shop, glancing up at Sera under his fringe of chin-length black hair. "We're just a bunch of pretty boys." He smiled playfully. "Especially me."

Sera raised her brows. I got the sudden impression that not only did she agree we were a group of lookers, but she also wasn't minding being stuck with us in the least.

"Speak for yourself," Liam snapped. His gaze didn't even flick my way, but I heard his next words clear as a bell within my mind. As the only shifters in our group, it was an intimacy we'd alone shared over the years. *"Why did we have to get stuck with Caden on this twisted adventure?"*

Caden's wry humor could get anyone's teeth on edge, and if he didn't curb his sass, the incubus just might get a wolfish throw down from Liam. By the look of it, Caden was looking for a good scrap. Or a good fuck. Often, with him, they were the same.

"Blame Franc," I replied. *"He continues to put up with the demon, no matter how poorly Caden behaves or what trouble he drags around."*

Liam huffed. *"I'd assume their on again, off again, liaisons have a lot to do with Franc's willingness to tolerate Caden's less desirable attributes."*

I shrugged. Who was I to nay say their fun? Especially considering that I worked security for Franc's club.

Franc held up his hand in warning to Caden, who shrugged his shoulders and then settled down. Then Franc turned to me. "Tell me more about Golden."

"I grew up here, but left with my dad when I was a teenager," I said, leaving out the dramatic backstory about my mom. I was a pretty private person, and it's not like we had time for a trip down memory lane anyway. "This is a typical Canadian mountain shifter town. Mostly panthers, like me. There's also a handful of bears and a sizable contingent of raptors who live further up the mountain. Hardly any humans, at least not that I remember."

"Any idea why Taneisha would have picked this place for your quest?" Sera asked me. "If we can understand her motivation, I think we'll have an easier time finding the Eye of the Tiger."

Beyond wanting to make me miserable, I thought about saying, but I held my tongue. I'd admired Sera's shrewd ability to break down problems in class. I'd trust her process now too.

"The legacy Taneisha stole from me was a carved soapstone black panther passed down from my mother after she died."

"My condolences. Losing a parent is tough," Sera said.

"Thank you. The panther is a symbol of the enduring spirit of our people," I explained. "I used it for meditation, but it's mostly sentimental."

"And now we're here, in the town you grew up in, surrounded by potential relatives?" she asked, and I nodded. "So there's the possibility your family might find out you lost your legacy to a fae?"

That hadn't occurred to me yet, but Sera was right. Even though I hadn't been back to Golden, I definitely didn't want the shame of them finding out I'd lost her legacy.

"I'd prefer they didn't, but mostly, I just need it back."

Sera stepped close, placing a comforting hand on my arm. "We'll get it back for you." The depth of emotion in her brown-eyed gaze stole my breath for a moment. I knew Sera understood what I wasn't saying: the soapstone panther was the last link I had to my mother.

"Enough standing around," Emrys said, his hands on his hips. "We need to find whoever has this Eye thing. Ideas?"

"I have one," Franc said. There was an older woman walking toward us on the sidewalk, and Franc caught her eye before swaggering over to her. "Hello, ma'am. Could I bother you for a moment?" he asked, flashing his best panty-dropping smile.

His charms were lost on the wizened lady. She crossed her arms and raised a brow, conspicuously sliding one hand inside the cavernous purse hung on her shoulder. I'd worked security long enough to know Franc would be lucky if she just pulled out a taser on him.

"Whadda you want?" she asked, eyeing him over, her hand still inside her purse. "Did you take a wrong turn off the freeway?"

Franc held up his hands while the rest of us stood where we were, smiled politely, and tried to look harmless. "You're right," he laughed. "I admit we're a little lost. My friend told us to find someone with the Eye of the Tiger. Do you know who she might have meant?"

Her face screwed up with irritation. "Is your friend daft or do they intentionally speak in riddles?"

Franc imitated a pair of scales with his hands. "Little of column A, little of column B... Any possibility you could help us out?"

She shook her head, taking her empty hand out of her purse and perching it on her hip instead. "Yeah, I think you're looking for Jasper Jeanneau. He can drone on about that Tiger Eye of his for as long as you'll let him."

"Oh my gods, thank you so much!" Franc turned to us. "Hey guys, aren't we lucky? The first person we met knows Jasper. See, this is going to be easy after all." He looked back at the lady, flashing her another smile. "What a coincidence. Tell me, do you know where we can find old Jasper?"

"He runs Pin Ticklers," she explained. The matron looked over our confused expressions and then continued.

"It's the bowling alley. One block south and three blocks west of here."

"Oh," Sera said, letting out a chuckle. "That was not where my brain went at that name."

Mine either. This was not the standoffish Sera I'd remembered from our academy days. This Sera was saucy, and yeah, I'd admit it, sexy.

"One more thing," Franc said. "Where's your nearest bar?"

The lady crossed her arms again. "Are you blind or just not trying that hard? Turn around and walk a few feet."

To be fair, I hadn't looked that way down the street either. The neon wine glass shining through the front window was definitely Franc's siren song.

"You've been such a help, ma'am. Thank you so much," Franc said.

The lady scurried off down the street, muttering "winos" under her breath. As she passed by, I caught a whiff of her scent. A wolf shifter? I didn't recall there being many here in my youth.

Franc sauntered over to me, his game face on. "Here's the plan, Marcos. I'm going to get a street-view seat at the bar and ask some questions. Get a lay of the land. If Tink shows up or I find out anything useful, I'll ping you on your phone to let you know what's going on."

I should have known Franc would pull this. He preferred to be the man behind the curtain, not the one out digging ditches.

"We should stick together," I replied. "You never know what tricks a fae has up her sleeve."

Franc nodded, his face masked with concern. "Precisely. Which is exactly why we shouldn't all be together, or we could end up stuck with no one to call for backup. It's lucky we're all here to each play the roles best suited to us."

I could keep pushing, but trying to change Franc's mind was like wrestling with an eel. I'd bet money Franc saw this challenge as being too easy, and thus beneath him.

"Fine. Who's with me to check out Pin Ticklers?" I asked, looking around at the rest of them. These were my closest friends, even though some of us had drifted apart. We'd been such a tight team at the academy, but a lot of time had passed since then. Old rivalries and a natural drift from spending less time together had worn at our once sure bonds.

Did they have it in them to come together and plow through Taneisha's challenges successfully? So far, it wasn't looking good.

"I'm in," Sera said, walking right on up to me, not sparing a single glance toward Franc. Despite being surrounded by a group of alpha males, Sera took control of the situation, seeming to feel no need to ask any of them permission. But why would she? As a mage from House Lowe, no doubt she was more powerful than any of us. Maybe even more powerful than all of us combined.

She slid her arm through mine, pulling on my jacket and tugging me along beside her. "Let's go."

I didn't look back at the others. I loved the feel of her body leaning against mine and the confidence with which Sera carried herself. I felt my panther fall into step, vigilant and focused, his purr rumbling through my thoughts.

Sera glanced up at me, frowning and smiling at the same time. "Are you... purring?"

That flirty look from her, and I felt my blood rush south. Yeah, I was purring in more ways than one. A smile tugged at the corner of my mouth. "Only on the inside."

"You always kept things close to your chest," she chuckled. "Tell me more about Golden?"

I didn't want to dwell on the past, but I understood Sera was trying to dig into Taneisha's motivation in picking this location, so I relented. "I grew up here, until I turned thirteen and my mom passed. My dad is mortal, and my mom's family had never accepted him or forgiven her for mating outside the supe community. He couldn't stomach staying in Golden after she died, not when they treated us like outsiders. So, we left."

We turned the corner, and I glanced back, seeing the others trailing behind us. Liam and Emrys were chatting, while Caden skulked along behind them.

Sera reached up with her free hand and absently scratched at her neck.

"Can you get a good look at that?" Liam asked me.

"Sure, but why?" I asked.

"It's just a hunch."

It was unlike Liam to hold back, but his instincts were usually spot on, so I didn't press him for more.

"That's a hell of a double trauma for you," Sera continued. "Losing your mom and your community in one blow. Have you been back since?"

"Nope," I said, hearing the curt edge in my tone. "My aunt and the rest of the family never so much as checked on me, came to visit, or invited me to stay with them."

"Ouch. How long after that until you spent time with other supes or shifters?"

I sighed. "Not until my days at Goldenbriar."

Sera shuddered against me, as if she'd caught a chill. I pulled her close, throwing an arm around her shoulders. "Hey, are you okay?" She nodded, and then another slight spasm shook her. Although if I hadn't been touching Sera, I might have missed it. "You sure? You don't seem okay."

Sera nodded again, but the anxious look in her eyes pulled at my heartstrings. "It happens sometimes, but it passes. It's nothing you need to worry about."

I caught the undercurrent Sera didn't say out loud, and understood that this was something that happened not occasionally, but often. I'd heard that some mages paid a heavy price for their magic. Could this be the case with Sera too? I'd ask, but her dismissive statement seemed to imply the topic wasn't open for discussion.

I hated to think of her suffering for her magic. Fate could be cruel sometimes.

We turned another corner and the sign for Pin Ticklers came into view. "Looks like we found it."

Emrys caught up with us, coming to walk next to Sera. "I hate to say it out loud, but this feels too easy," Emrys said.

Had things ever been difficult for Emrys?

Sera released my arm, and I felt my panther's hackles raise. My beast and I both wanted Sera to remain by our side. Suddenly, Emrys felt like competition. *That was a first.* Sure, he was a quintessential ladies' man, dating someone new every week. I rarely dated, but not for lack of interest or availability. I just felt like I'd been waiting for the right woman, not just whomever was in the club that day.

"Don't go looking for trouble, Em," I replied.

"No, I agree with Em," Sera said. "Taneisha gave us all

day to find the Eye for her. I'd bet it won't be smooth sailing with Jasper."

I mulled that over as I moved forward and pulled open the door to the bowling alley. Sera was right. Taneisha had stolen our legacies to mess with us. Taneisha was also a fae. Therefore, fuckery would be afoot.

Caden clucked at me as he passed by. "You're not our doorman, Marcos."

I shook my head, following him into the building. "Don't sass me, demon."

I thought I caught a pained look in Caden's eyes, but it quickly transformed into a look of stoic resignation. "Whatever. Have it your way, kitty cat."

I gritted my teeth but tamped down my desire to snap back at him. Even if the timing had been better, the incubus wasn't about to listen to me.

The bowling alley was pretty quiet, but then, it was a small town. An older, grizzled man with a touch of gray in his beard sat behind the main counter, spraying antifungal into shoes, as he watched maybe a dozen patrons bowl and throw back beers.

Liam and Caden hung back while Sera strode right up to the counter, Emrys at her side. Wanting to be involved in the discussion, I moved forward and joined them at the counter.

"Hello, do you know where we can find Jasper Jeanneau?" Sera asked.

The man stood, and I instantly recognized him as a bear shifter. I guessed he might even be the local patriarch, too, by the way he carried himself. Burly, tall, and solid as a boulder, I wouldn't have wanted to square off against him. Despite his years, I'd wager he could more than hold his own.

"You've found him. You's all can stay, but the demon has got to go."

Caden rolled his eyes. "Whatever, mister creaky cranky pants."

Jasper raised a brow. "Boy, I could chew you up and spit you out."

Caden smirked, and then headed out the door. "That's what she said. Or was it he said? Whatever. I'll be out front when you guys, and gal, need me. Which I know, is always."

I'd hand it to him. The incubus might have a knack for finding trouble, but lacking in confidence, he was not.

"Now, what can I do you for?" Jasper asked.

"We're looking for something and were told you might know about it," I said. "It's called the Eye of the Tiger."

Jasper set down the shoe he was polishing and crossed his arms. "Are you now?" he asked, the tone of his voice challenging them.

Em, Sera, and I exchanged cautious glances, but it was Sera who answered Jasper. "Yes, an associate of ours asked us to see about acquiring it for her. Do you still have it?"

A sly grin spread across Jasper's wizened face. He looked at each of us again, as if he was measuring our mettle. "Yeah, I do." Without turning around, he pointed to a glass case to his right, full of bowling balls.

Only then did I notice the one in the center, the only one without a price tag. It was a little smaller than the other balls, but its tiger-stripe colors swirled and moved, iridescent and casting a barely noticeable glow.

"Is that a bowling ball?" I asked.

Jasper's disappointed frown was my answer. "Heck no, but it looks mighty fine in there. Don't cha think?"

"It's a truly impressive specimen," Sera answered him, her voice full of praise. Standing up on the balls of her feet, she leaned on the counter to get a better look at the Eye. My attention was drawn not to the orb, but to the shapely curve of her ass bent over that counter. I suddenly needed to adjust myself. "I've never seen one. What's it do?"

"Well, you see here, it's an oracular orb. Whoever holds it sees any troubles coming their way."

"Wow. Does it work for anyone?" she asked.

"Uh-huh. But I don't let just anyone look at it, you understand?"

"Sure," Sera said. She leaned in again, cocking her head to the side. "I bet someone like you doesn't even need something like the Eye. I doubt any shifter would stand up to you, much less fight you for it."

Jasper let out a chuckle. "Well, now, you're right on the mark there."

Sera sure was laying it on thick, and although I understood she was trying to play into Jasper's good graces, her words ruffled my fur. I wanted to step up behind her, pull her against me, and bite down on the tender flesh of her neck just hard enough to tell her she was mine.

I froze. Woah. I gave my head a little shake. What was that all about? Why was I acting this way toward Sera?

"Hold, brother." I heard Liam's voice in my head. He was leaning against the counter beside us. *"Your eyes are flashing green,"* he said to me, a sheen of yellow painting

his eyes, a sign of his wolf rising, fighting for control. *"Now would be a bad time to lose control."*

I gave him a curt nod, turning my attention back to Jasper. Why were both of our beasts clawing at the surface? Perhaps it was some fae magic Taneisha used to keep us off balance?

"How much do you want for it?" Sera asked, all smiles for the old bear.

"Yeah, it surely is impressive, but it's not for sale, I'm afraid." As Jasper sat back down in his chair, it creaked a little under his weight.

Sera's hopeful expression fled, and her shoulders sagged. "No? That's too bad. Are you sure there's nothing that might convince you to part with it?"

Scratching at his beard, Jasper looked her over, sniffing deeply. "There is one thing, but it's beyond your reach. No one's been able to crack that egg."

"Humor us?" Emrys said. "We're more resourceful than you think at egg cracking."

Jasper's brows raised. Emrys looked so earnest, the old bear seemed to decide the demigod was being genuine. "Alrighty then. There is one thing, and one thing only, that'd I'd trade my Eye for. The Altruscan Orchid."

I had a sinking feeling in the pit of my stomach. "The what?" I asked.

"You really aren't from around here, are you?" Jasper asked. I shook my head, as did the others. "At the other end of Main Street, there's a garden nursery run by Amber Watson, called Ferns and Things. That doll can grow anything, you know what I mean? Well, she takes in strays sometimes."

"Stray... plants?" Sera asked.

He nodded vigorously. "It's not so weird. Sometimes plants just don't like certain homes. Or certain peoples." He winked at her. "Amber rehabilitates them, gets them back up on their stalks, so to speak. Anyway, she's got an orchid I've been trying to talk her out of for years." It was Jasper's turn to lean in, and he whispered. "The blooms from that orchid guarantee a blissful night's sleep, you see."

"You'd trade foreseeing threats for restful sleep?" Emrys said, his voice incredulous. A moment later Sera's foot came down on his, and Emrys froze, biting his lip.

Atta gal. I liked her style.

"Hell, yeah," Jasper shot back. "I can tell you don't appreciate proper sleep, son. If I had that bloomin' orchid, it'd be bye-bye restless legs. Bye-bye nightmares. I'd wake up every day refreshed and perky. Now that's worth a million dollars. Or, one Eye, as it were."

Sera held out her hand to Jasper. "One Altruscan Orchid for the Eye of the Tiger. Deal?"

Jasper didn't hesitate. He took Sera's hand and gave it a firm shake. "Best of luck, little lady. You're gonna need it."

MORE LIKE A SWAP MEET
SERA

As I walked in the nursery's direction with Marcos close by my side, I couldn't shake the thought that something was off with my magic. Like, more than normal. Extra-special off. My power was straining at the seams, the sensation of micro-sparks of electricity buzzing against my skin, occasionally peaking to shooting pain. It made sense, because I hadn't had my daily wear myself out session at the gym, and yet this felt like more.

Something new was going on. I just had to figure out what. At least I hadn't needed to make a magely display of power. So far.

No doubt Taneisha was behind my magic being off balance. She'd kept me here for a reason, I was sure of it. But why? I'd have to figure that part out later. I couldn't help scratching my shoulder again.

"What's going on with your shoulder?" Marcos asked.

"I don't know. My skin keeps itching. It started when we were in Faery, so I'm blaming Taneisha."

"Can I have a look?" he asked.

"Yeah, sure, why not?" Without slowing down, I pulled the neck of my shirt off to the side, exposing my shoulder.

Marcos hesitated, and then reached over and ran his fingertips across my skin, moving my long raven hair out of the way. My nerve endings lit up under his touch, the contact soothing the frayed, sharp edges of the magic coursing through my body.

Woah. He totally needed to stop that. Like, an hour from now. Maybe two.

Reveling in the moment, I almost missed the look of confusion that passed over Marcos' face. "Crap, what is it?" He pulled away, lost in thought, and I smoothed out my shirt. "No, really, Marcos. Is it a rash or something?"

He hesitated, but then spoke. "It's not a rash. More like a symbol or a mark, but I'm not sure what it means."

I had a gut feeling he was holding back, but that might have just been because he didn't know what the mark meant. "I bet Taneisha knows. When I showed her, she didn't seem surprised at all."

"We'll get it figured out. I promise you, Seraphina Lowe."

Marcos was so earnest. Even using my full name. I almost laughed. But he wasn't laughing, so I sobered up quickly. I reminded myself that Taneisha had refused to send me home to punish me for helping the guys. No doubt the mark meant trouble.

Emrys moved closer, falling into step on the other side of me, and breaking the spell of the moment. "What do you two think of this turn of events with the orchid lady?"

"Odds are, she'll demand payment too. I assume you guys have your wallets handy?" I asked.

Emrys ran a hand through his hair. "This could get expensive. There's only so many favors I can hand out."

"You mean before your family takes note. Does your mom keep a list of every outstanding debt?" Marcos asked.

"As a matter of fact, Grandma does."

Ouch... "Oh, you don't want to chap her hide. She'll put you in the ground for a few months to teach you a lesson," I said, intending it as a joke.

When Emrys blanched, I regretted my words. But then he forced a smile and barked out a laugh. "What's a little resurrection between friends and family?"

Marcos shook his head. "That's fucked up, is what it is, man."

"You guys are really smooth with the ladies," Caden said. "Yet despite your poor form, you're still monopolizing the lady. I really should take notes."

I glanced back, watching Liam and Caden walking side by side behind us. "You can't monopolize a person." Despite Caden's snark, Liam's brooding attention was all over me. Shivering under the intensity of his focus, I refocused forward.

"Not all of us can rely on demonic persuasion to get things done," Em quipped back, flashing me a smile full of overconfidence. "Some of us have had to work on our charm. Not that I'd call it work." He winked again.

I rolled my eyes at Emrys. "You were definitely more charming before you got me stuck in Faery."

He feigned shock, which shouldn't have been adorable, but somehow, it still was. Worse, the back and forth was riling me, and therefore my magic, up. I could feel the power crackling at my fingertips. What would happen if it burst out uncontrolled? With all of us together, someone would notice if my magic went haywire. And then what would I do?

"Enough chitter chatter and flirtatious banter. What's our plan with the flower lady?" Caden asked.

"As if you didn't start it?" Marcos growled at him.

I stopped short and spun around, holding up my hands. "Stop it, all of you." An ominous, if timely, crackle of electricity ran across my fingertips. Whoops? "We need someone to go to Franc and update him."

None of them appeared deterred by my minor display of power. Emrys didn't even seem to notice, while curiosity lit up Liam's features. Caden's lips parted, and his brow arched as he drew in a quick breath. I had the distinct impression he was thinking about the lascivious potential of my sparks, which, oh my goodness, I'd never thought of before. Now that he'd planted the idea in my mind, I couldn't help but wonder about it.

"I could call him?" Marcos offered.

I dropped my hands to my hips. "No. I don't think we should trust phones. It'd be too easy for Taneisha to mimic our voices in a conversation," I said, and Marcos nodded in agreement. "Who's going to go?"

Caden sighed dramatically. "I'll find Franc and let him know you're all out shopping for flowers."

"No," Marcos said. "We're all in this together. Tell him he needs to be here helping, not sitting on his butt, day drinking."

"I think he gets special dispensation?" Caden replied. "On the drinking, I mean. Wine god, and all that?"

"Please, Caden," Emrys said. "Take this seriously. Franc will listen to you."

This time, Caden's smile was genuine, but his finger

guns made me chuckle. "True. I'll be back. Don't get rowdy without me."

As if that was going to happen? But then, as I looked from Emrys to Liam to Marcos, I didn't think I'd kick any of them out of bed for eating crackers.

LIAM

"You're not making sense." I clenched my jaw. *"Describe the mark again,"* I demanded of Marcos telepathically.

"I told you. There's a mating mark on her right shoulder, I'm sure of it."

After arriving at the garden nursery, the front staff directed us to the greenhouse at the far end of the lot. We walked between rows of saplings. Emrys and Sera were in the lead, while I walked side by side with Marcos, a few paces behind them.

It took an effort to draw my gaze away from Sera. Emrys kept touching her back or arm, and each time, my wolf urged me forward, as if he wanted to separate them. I'd felt similarly when she was walking next to Marcos, but my wolf's reaction hadn't been as strong. Now? I couldn't imagine leaving her presence.

I wanted my hand on the small of her back. Wanted the heat of her body pressed against my own. Her scent on my skin.

I shook my head, trying to stay focused. *"What kind of shifter mark?"*

Marcos rubbed the back of his neck and then shrugged. *"I'm not sure."*

How ridiculous. *"I don't get it, man. You saw it. How can you not know?"*

"I'm not sure what I saw. It reminded me of panther spots, but they didn't look right. I need another look. She's been scratching her left shoulder, too, but I didn't get a look at that side."

My wolf's hackles raised. *"Is it a mating mark?"* I asked Marcos, but it was my wolf who answered me.

Mine.

An image of me sinking my teeth into Sera's shoulder, claiming her as my own, flooded my mind.

Yeah, yeah, big guy. Simmer down.

While my wolf seemed certain, I didn't know what to make of his declaration. I'd thought the beast recognized its mate the first time they met, yet I'd known Sera back at academy and this was the first sign my wolf had given of interest in her. Sure, I'd been attracted to her. Respected her independence and strength. Been intrigued by her mystique and magic, despite never seeing her in action. But never had my wolf insisted on having a claim to her.

At least, not until now.

"Maybe? I need a better look," Marcos replied.

"We'll both have a better look."

Marcos arched a brow, a sly smile curling his lips. *"My panther has opinions. What's your wolf saying?"*

Interesting. His beast was also laying claim? Could we *both* be mated to Sera?

I looked at Marcos again, sizing him up in a new light. Had fate paired us together with the mage? I'd never heard of such a thing, but fate could be capricious. If both of our beasts claimed her, and she accepted us, where would that leave us?

At least I respected Marcos and already considered him family. Hell, we'd dated women together during our days at the academy. At least it wasn't the demon, Caden. That would have been literal, and figurative, hell. I might consider Caden a brother, but he was the 'perpetually in trouble and down on his luck' brother who always needed something. Like being bailed out of jail.

"My wolf has opinions too," I admitted. Marcos let out a low whistle as he digested my admission. *"However, I am suspicious that the marks surfaced once we entered Faery together. What if it's a fae trick to pit us against each other?"*

"No one can fake mating marks," Marcos said. *"No one can force fate, especially not a singular, if troublesome, fae."*

"Agreed. However, Taneisha saw the marks on Sera. I'm sure the fae plans to use whatever means available to make our lives more difficult. We need to find out what Sera is experiencing and get a better look at her shoulders."

Marcos nodded.

When we reached the greenhouse, Emrys opened the door, ushering Sera inside first. He waited for Marcos and me to catch up, holding the door open for us as well.

"What have you two been chatting about?" Emrys tapped his forehead with his free hand. "Your silence has been deafening."

"When you need to know, you'll know," Marcos replied.

Emrys put his hand on my chest, bringing me up short. "I'd prefer to know now. Something is going on between you two. Besides, it serves none of us to keep secrets on this quest."

Sera appeared at the door, stepping outside to talk to us. "What's the holdup, buttercups?"

Oh, how I wanted to taste and nibble on that full, pouty lower lip of hers.

Emrys removed his hand from my chest. "They won't tell me, but they were discussing something."

"It's just guy stuff. We'd have shared if it was important to you, Em," I replied.

Emrys glowered at me. He'd never been good at taking a joke or being left out.

Sera's brows knit in consternation as she turned to Marcos and then me. She gave us a single terse nod. "I'm sure if it was critical to finding Marcos' legacy or the others, you'd have included the rest of us in your conversation. Let's worry about it later, Em. We have a gardener to sweet talk."

She turned and walked back inside, and this time Marcos was on her heels. I admired how decisive Sera was, and how she handled Emrys without coddling his ego or fawning all over him like I'd seen so many women do over the years.

Emrys just stood there, digging in his heels.

I put my hand on his shoulder. "It's shifter stuff, Em. It's not personal nor about you, difficult as that might be for you to believe."

"Fine," he said, his tone curt.

We followed the others inside, and my sensitive wolf senses were assaulted by a miasma of floral perfume. Having a wolf's nose was usually a benefit, but not right now it wasn't.

"Holy hells," I said to Marcos mentally. But then, remembering Sera's earlier statement about not having private conversations, I continued out loud. "I can't be the only shifter in town that finds this place…"

"Intolerable?" Marcos finished for me.

Sera turned back and held up a warning finger toward us. "Shh!" I swear she had no right to look so adorable as she shushed us. A spark of green flame flashed from her fingertip. Concern furrowed her brows, and I heard a quick intake of breath as Sera rubbed her hands together and then folded her arms across her midsection.

What was going on? Was something wrong with Sera? A combination of my concern and my wolf's urging moved me forward to walk alongside Sera, with Marcos on the other side of her.

I was about to ask Sera if she was okay when a stately woman turned onto our row, wielding a pair of serious-looking pruning shears. From her stance and the shears, I suspected we'd interrupted her work. The flash of her green eyes paired with gray-tinged auburn hair, and pale, freckled skin marked her likely Irish lineage. Her scent declared her a wolf shifter.

"Are you Amber Watson?" Sera asked, once again taking the lead.

The lady's gaze lingered over us, and me in particular, for a few moments before she answered. "Yeah, that'd be me. How can I help you?"

"We're hoping you might have an Altruscan Orchid available?" Sera asked.

Amber looked them over again before answering. "You're a strange lot, but you look healthy enough. What would you need with my orchid?"

"We've got a friend who isn't sleeping well," Marcos replied. "Thought we'd gift him something to help."

Amber crossed her arms and arched her brow. "Is that friend's name Jasper?"

"If the flower's for sale, what does it matter?" I asked.

Amber sniffed deliberately in my direction and then made a face like she'd smelled something foul. "Who's your pack, wolf?"

I hesitated. Entering another pack's territory unannounced could lead to trouble, but there was no helping it now. "I'm with the Leblanc pack in British Columbia. My friends and I are just passing through town today. I didn't know there was a pack in town, or I would have announced myself."

Amber's brow arched. "Fair enough. Let me get this straight. You've come into town for just the day, and yet somehow, you're already running errands for old Jasper?"

Emrys didn't appear able to help himself. He sauntered around Marcos, his intent to dazzle Amber obvious from his swagger and sultry smile.

"Are you sure you can't help us out, Ms. Watson?" he drawled. A light flush spread over her cheeks, and I noticed the slightest hint of a green glow in her eyes. "We'd be so grateful, and we're happy to compensate you for your troubles."

From his tone, I wondered if more than simply money was on the table. Emrys had always been an incorrigible flirt, and today was no different. I sighed, unable under the strain of the day to keep my frustration from surfacing. When Emrys got serious about a woman, he'd discover these tricks wouldn't work. But what did I care?

I glanced at Sera, whose irritation was pouring off her in energetic waves as she watched Emrys try to flirt with Amber. I wasn't usually this sensitive to the emotional auras of those around me. Perhaps it was because of the fae magic which had thrust us into this quest together.

Amber stepped closer to Emrys. For a moment, I thought he had her hooked. Sera must have too, because tendrils of green fire erupted from her hands, which she had fisted at her sides.

"Just how much are you willing to part with for my pretty flowers?" Amber asked, snapping the shears open and closed just a little too close to Emrys' groin.

"Not that much!" Emrys jumped backward, knocking over some plants on the shelf behind him in his bid to avoid Amber's pruning shears, which she kept snapping shut in his direction.

"Amber," Sera said, interrupting them. Her hands were still aflame, but she held them, fingers threaded together behind her back. "I mean Ms. Watson. Please forgive Emrys. Despite being a demigod, he's got more looks than sense."

Amber backed off Emrys and walked back over to us. "You've got that right. And you are?"

"I'm Seraphina Lowe, mage. You're right, we weren't straight with you."

Amber's chin raised. "I have a nose for these things. Go on."

Sera nodded. "We are on a quest, of sorts, and need to get the Eye of the Tiger from Jasper. He'll part with it, but only for your Altruscan Orchid."

"So, you're not friends of his?"

"Nope, we just met him an hour ago."

"Oh, well then. And what do you need his Eye for?"

"Nothing," Sera replied. As they'd talked, the flames in her hands had died down, just now dying out. "A fae has demanded it of us and will destroy something of Marcos' if we don't get it to her by noon tomorrow," Sera explained, gesturing to Marcos when she said his name.

"Those damned fae." Amber shook her head. "I've had my altercations with them myself, so you have my sympathies." With her free hand, she thumbed her chin.

"Since you're being straight with me now, I'll be straight with you. Here's the deal. I've been trying everything to propagate that orchid, and I've finally had some luck."

"That's fantastic, congratulations," Sera replied. "Does that mean you have some for sale?"

"Well," Amber replied. "I have a couple of keikis, those are baby orchids, which are coming along. One is even big enough that it's close to blooming."

"That sounds perfect. How much do you want for it?" Sera asked.

Watching Sera handle Amber, a sense of pride and admiration washed over me. She was always the cleverest girl in class, but seeing her step into a charged situation, take control, and turn it around was its own sort of magic. She'd even reined in her magic, despite being on the edge a few minutes ago.

Amber smiled. "I don't want your money. What I need is pixie poop."

"Did you just say pixie poop?" Emrys said, rejoining the conversation.

"Look, I've tried, but it's hard for a shifter like myself to get. The pixies smell me coming and bolt."

"Why do you need it?" Sera asked.

Amber's face lit up. "It's the best fertilizer, and it's the only one that will force these Altruscan Orchids to flower and make little baby plants. I ran out a few weeks ago, so this is serendipity that you all came along."

"Lucky us. Don't pixies bite?" Marcos asked.

"Oh yes. Venomous too. But I'm sure by working together you can outsmart the little pests and get me what I need. And when I have what I need, you can have your flower. For Jasper, right?"

"Right," Sera replied. "Okay, we'll do it. Is there a local pixie hangout you'd recommend for this endeavor?"

Amber nodded vigorously, pulled a notepad and pen out of her pocket, and scratched out an address. "Try here. It's a spot a little way out of town in a protected supernatural wilderness habitat. There's a visitor center and everything. You can't miss it."

Amber held out the note and Sera took it. Sera offered her hand. They shook on it, and the deal was made.

"We'll be back first thing in the morning, so plan to be here early."

"I'd stay up all night for a chance at pixie poop. Good luck!" Amber said, waving us goodbye.

THE RUNAROUND
SERA

Not having a car, we walked across town, down a nature trail path, and across a wide bridge to reach the visitor's center. I couldn't help but keep in mind how long everything was taking us to navigate, knowing we'd have to retrace our steps to get back to the orchid, and then the Eye, in order to meet Taneisha's deadline of noon tomorrow.

I'd called Pepper three times, but it always went straight to voicemail. Fae magic, no doubt. On the third go, I left Pepper a message saying Emrys had whisked me out of town for a few days, which was totally honest, and that I trusted her to manage the shop while I was gone. I had to hope Taneisha would allow the message to go through.

Marcos and Liam had been on either side of me most of the way, with a quiet Emrys scouting ahead of us. They were so protective; it was as if they'd expected resistance or an attack at any moment. I had a moment where I thought they were all vying to walk next to me, but that couldn't be right. Could it?

I didn't have their stakes in this joint venture, but so far, this puzzle had been pretty easy to navigate. Just a lot of negotiations and running around. Then again, Taneisha had said she wasn't as pissed at Marcos as the others. Hopefully, it would just be more of the same.

Eh, I was lucky, but that lucky? Not likely.

The wilderness visitor's center had a general population section with a gift store, maps section, and history dioramas. As we strolled through the dioramas, Liam pointed out a Staff Only sign on what looked to be a utility closet. From the glowing magic on the words, I knew it was an invitation for paranormals like us to explore further.

As we watched videos on wetland birds and waited for the sightseeing human family in the room to move on to the next section, Liam, Marcos, and Emrys circled around me, each lost in their own thoughts. They reminded me of sharks circling their prey. Did they even realize they were doing it?

With all of that male attention focused my way, a wicked thrill shot through me. My gaze lingered on Liam, who was the one directly in front of me. His frame had bulked out since I'd last seen him. His shoulders were broader than I'd remembered, and he'd grown out his ginger hair and added a short-cropped beard, which fit his severe features. I'd bet money he did something physical for work versus a desk job.

His green-eyed gaze met mine, his hint of a smile and arched brow let me know Liam had seen me giving him the once-over. There was a heat in his eyes that said he'd appreciated being the center of my attention. But the moment was short-lived. When his gaze narrowed and flicked down to my hands, I realized only then that a flicker of mage fire covered my fingertips.

How had I not noticed my magic leaking out? Worse, Liam had. I immediately crossed my arms, hiding my hands up against my body. Neither Marcos nor Emrys were looking at me. Perhaps only Liam had seen it?

Liam came over and leaned close to me. "Are you okay?" he whispered.

I nodded, leaning around him to get a look at the humans in the room. "Did they notice?"

He shook his head. "Does that happen a lot?"

I shrugged. There was no use denying it. I knew he meant how my mage fire just appeared. He must have seen it earlier at Amber's nursery, as he'd been standing behind me.

"I usually do daily exercises, but with this outing, I'm off my normal schedule."

"Oh, well, of course. I've heard mages spend a great deal of time meditating and focusing on their energy. So you need some focused quiet time to rebalance?"

I'd meant just exercise but appreciated his offer. "Yeah, that'd be great. Maybe when we get outside later?"

"Whatever you need," Liam replied, his voice smooth as silk over my skin. "I know you agreed to come along and help us, but that street goes both ways. If you need our help with anything, just ask."

The shiver that ran through me had nothing to do with being cold, and by Liam's sexy smile, I knew he knew the effect he'd had on me.

Emrys walked up to us. "Are you cold? Do you need a jacket?" he said, offering his coat.

Were they fighting for my attention? It was unexpected, and I sort of loved it. Was that wrong?

"I'm fine, just eager for the humans to leave," I replied.

Emrys nodded. "I have this gut feeling, but I'm sure Tin... Taneisha has made this task impossible."

Had he always been this cynical, or was it just the circumstances that had brought it out in Emrys? "Just because the fae are known for being tricksters, doesn't mean she's rigged her puzzles," I replied.

"Why wouldn't she? She clearly wants to see us suffer. So why not?" Emrys said.

"Either she's rigged it, or she hasn't," Marcos said. "We can't know either way, so we have to proceed under the assumption that she's not and that we can get our legacies back."

"Exactly. Can you try to call Franc and Caden again?" I asked Emrys. "We can use everyone's help to gather poop."

Emrys smiled. "Yeah, wouldn't want them to feel left out, would we?"

I noticed when he dialed, someone answered right away, unlike my earlier attempts to call Pepper. Damned Taneisha.

The humans moved on, and then Liam opened the Staff Only door and we all went through.

The layout of the supernatural-friendly exhibits was like what we'd seen so far, but here there were pictures of sprites and pixies. There was even an interactive exhibit with a remote. You could drive a tiny, camouflaged rover around the wetlands, picking up debris and trash to protect native habitats. There was a lone technician working inside a lab with a panoramic window, who looked up and waved hello at our arrival.

Emrys approached the rover's controls with single-minded focus, at first testing out the rover's motion and then popping a wheelie before zooming it around the enclosure.

"You look amused with yourself," I said.

"I can drive anything with an engine." He winked at me. "And we're supposed to be playing the role of tourists, right?"

When the rover spun round a corner, the lights in the enclosure flickered. A wee pixie with a tuft of bright yellow hair emerged from an earthen mound surrounded by reeds and tall grasses, chasing the little rover.

Marcos chuckled. "Uh-oh, it looks like you've awakened the kraken."

"Kraken are a myth," Emrys replied.

The little pixie shot lightning from her hands, stalling out the rover.

Emrys yelped, pulling his hands away from the controls. "It shocked me!"

"I don't actually think the kraken are a myth," Liam replied.

Emrys just rolled his eyes at him. "Don't you start. There's no recent evidence, so they might as well be a myth."

The technician emerged from his lab cave to talk with us, catching that last bit of conversation. His name tag read 'Greyson.' Living in a predominately supe community, I figured he was a shifter too. "It's ironic to hear a supe dismissing cryptids."

"Just because they're in folklore doesn't mean they're real," Emrys replied. "What's with the shocks?"

Greyson's brows rose, and he seemed taken aback.

"Folklore research has long been a standard for discovering the long-forgotten supernatural truths of various cultures. And the shocks are haptic feedback I thought made the experience more real. What do you think?"

Emrys frowned at him. "I could do without it."

"Ah well, to each their own," Greyson replied.

"Was that a real pixie?" I asked, endeavoring to build the conversation with the tech. We needed to know as much about pixies as possible if we were to complete this stage in the fae's puzzle.

Greyson gave me a double take. "No. No, of course it's not real. The pixie figure you see is illusory. We'd never endanger a real pixie or force one into confinement."

"Oh, I mean, of course not," I replied, smiling over at him. Then I continued, hoping to stroke his ego and get him talking. "You're here to protect them, not exploit them. What kind of conservationist work does the habitat do for pixies?"

Greyson puffed his chest up and raised his chin, exuding confidence. He was fit, but not anywhere near as built as the boys. Posse? I needed to come up with a name for them.

"This center was established about forty years ago, when locals discovered the native sprite and pixie populations," Greyson explained. "We discovered that the city and local manufacturing was impacting the wetlands, and thus, also the pixies. Based on our research, key chemicals have been banned from use and light pollution has been reduced."

"That's fascinating, Greyson. I see you have a lab? What are you working on?"

He smiled at my praise. "We've been studying pixie diets to understand what they eat."

"How do you do that?" I asked.

"Well, in part, we take samples of the wildlife in the area. Bugs, plants, and the like. Then we collect droppings and run an analysis of the compounds."

"You mean you collect their poop?" Marcos asked.

Ding! Ding! Ding! Just what we needed!

"Yes," Greyson replied. "But we use every precaution. It's why I only work with it under a laminar flow hood. Also, the preserve has a license to collect and study it, otherwise it'd be illegal to have pixie droppings in this quantity."

Illegal? Amber had conveniently left that out of her request. I supposed we'd have to make sure and only take her a little? "A lamin-what?" I asked, letting out a giggle.

Liam, who was standing to one side of the technician, raised a brow at my behavior. Yeah, I wasn't ditzy, but if it got Greyson talking, I could play naive long enough.

"It's an air-controlled box which pulls away stray particles into a filter, so I don't accidentally breathe any in. Plus, I use special shielded gloves."

"So you're saying pixie poop is dangerous?" Marcos asked, his face deadly serious.

"Yes, but you don't need to worry. If you ever came across it in the wild, it would most likely be diluted enough not to cause ill effects," Greyson replied. "That's why we only allow observers to view the wetlands at a safe distance, and never at night."

Which was exactly what we'd planned to do.

"What could happen if the box failed you?" I asked. "Could it hurt you?" We needed to know what dangers we were facing in transporting it. Dangers Amber had also failed to mention.

"Well, often an electrical charge is still present on the droppings. There's recorded instances of people being knocked out or having heart attacks from the strength of the discharge. Supes, even."

Lightning death via pixie poop. Got it.

"Wow, that's scary," I replied, holding a hand up to cover my mouth. "How late are you open?"

Greyson glanced at the wall clock. "Only another thirty minutes. I'll leave you to observe. I encourage you to take a walk out along the deck. If you're lucky, sometimes you can catch glimpses of the sprites in the distance this close to dusk. Have fun and let me know if you all have any more questions."

As he walked away, I pointed to the door to the deck outside. "Shall we?" Once outside, we walked up to the banister, alone with the sounds of croaking frogs and something rustling in the reeds nearby. The guys circled me again. I suspected it wasn't intentional. Just them being as close to me as possible while still giving each other space.

"I'm thinking our next step is finding a place out here to hide until the visitor center shuts down for the day," I said. "Then we can go hunting for a pixie toilet. Thoughts?"

"Greyson said he had a supply of the stuff," Emrys replied. "We could always take some of his?"

Liam shook his head. "We can't. The rules of the fae's puzzle were clear. No stealing."

"The alternative is tromping through the muck all night, dealing with aggressive pixies, and risking ourselves," Emrys said. "If we're careful, Greyson won't even notice any missing. Amber didn't specify a quantity, just that she needed 'some,'" he explained, the last word with his hands miming air quotes.

"No, Liam is correct," Marcos replied. "Also, this is too dangerous for all of you, especially you, Sera. So I'm doing this one on my own. There's no point putting us all in danger."

I pushed away from the banister and moved close to Marcos, pushing my index finger up against his chest. "What the hell are you going on about? We're all in this together now, right?"

Marcos put his hands on his hips. "This job is too dangerous for you, little mage. I won't risk you."

His words stirred something in me. Something primal. Yet I wasn't about to sit this one out, no matter how adoringly protective these men were of me.

"There's nothing little about me," I shot back. "It's not up to you whether I take risks." Marcos crossed his arms, and a flash of yellow lit up his eyes, but it vanished a moment later. "I'm up to this task, Marcos. Besides, we need everyone pitching in for this to work. For all we know, every puzzle will get harder as we go. We need to use this trial to get closer and work together. Let it strengthen us, instead of dividing us."

"She's right, Marcos," Liam replied. "We have to work together if we hope to win against the fae."

"We're all in this together, man," Emrys chimed in. "No one is walking away and leaving you to go solo."

Marcos sighed, defeated. "Fine, so where do you propose we hide out?"

"Well, there's a shed over there we could check out. We

just need to make the staff think we've left," I said. "Emrys, could you make a distracting and charming show of heading out, and then circle back around?"

Humor glinted in his eyes as Emrys ran a hand through his hair, and then his gaze raked over me. Memory of him leaning over me against those racks flashed through my mind again.

"I thought you said we should stick together?" Emrys asked.

"That's why I suggested you circle back around after you put them off your scent. Okay?"

Was Emrys grousing over me calling the shots? He hesitated, but finally nodded. "Fine. I'll call Franc and Caden too. If we're going to tromp through the swamp together, they will not miss out on that fun."

OUTLAW RULES
EMRYS

I couldn't shake the feeling that leaving Liam and Marcos alone with Sera right now was the exact wrong move. There was something in the dynamic between them that had me on edge. I couldn't blame the others for finding Sera attractive, but hell, I was the one who brought her into these shenanigans. Didn't that give me dibs to pursue her?

Not that anyone could tell Sera what to do. Headstrong, sassy, and a born leader. Just like I remembered her from the academy. Those same qualities had memories of Sera sneaking into my thoughts and fantasies regularly.

Remembering our moments together earlier, alone in the back room at her work, my shaft went hard. If I'd had time, I would have made my move. Sera had been receptive, that much I was sure of. She'd have opened to me like a flower.

Damn Tink and damn her ridiculous puzzles.

Wandering back through the supe area of the exhibits, I pulled out my phone and called Franc.

"'Sup?" he answered.

"Enjoying your preferred vintage?"

"I'm not always that predictable," Franc replied, his voice a slow drawl. "They had an amazing small batch whiskey I couldn't pass up."

"Meaning they're all out of wine?"

Franc scoffed. "I have a policy against house jug wine. But tell me, what trouble are you all up to? Has the fae been showing up to heckle you too?"

I laughed. "Nope, just you. Have you learned anything new from Tink?"

"I can report that her laugh-cackle is no less irritating. Otherwise, no. It's been unusually quiet here, for the town bar."

"Good. We need your help down at a nature reserve to gather pixie poop."

There was a pause on the line, and I thought I heard ice clinking. "I'm not sure psychedelics are the best choice right now, brother."

"I'm not high. It's just..." I groaned. "Complicated. We've arranged a series of trades, and for the last item, we have to tromp through a swamp, at night, raiding pixie toilets."

"You always did know how to party," Franc replied. "Aren't pixies dangerous?"

"Only if you're not into electroshock treatments," I sighed. Even Franc recognized the difficulty ahead of us. "I'm really not sure this task is even possible. But get down here and bring Caden with you. He's there, right?"

"He is, although he just got here. Thus, why I was surprised to get your call."

"Huh. Caden must have gotten waylaid? We sent him over a while back."

I could almost hear Franc smile. "Demons will be demons. Send me your location and we'll head over."

"See you soon." I hung up, hoping Caden wasn't causing too much trouble.

"Hey there, you're still here?" Greyson said from behind me. "We're a couple minutes to closing."

I spun around and flashed the habitat tech what I hoped was a nonchalant smile. "I had a call I was finishing up. Are you heading out?"

"Yes, it's been a long day. I could walk out with you?"

"Yeah, sure." All the better for him to think we'd all left. Mostly, I just needed to make sure he didn't go out on the viewing deck in case the others weren't hidden yet.

"Oh, just a moment, I need to get my things."

I knew the rules of the fae's game, but I couldn't help taking advantage of opportunities that presented themselves. Besides, we all knew Tink would not make the puzzles solvable. If I could find an easier route, or a way around her rules, what would it hurt anyone? The key was in skirting her rules while crossing no lines.

I slid off my jacket and laid it on a nearby bench before I caught up with Greyson as he reentered his lab. I caught the door and held it open, leaning against the frame.

"Do you usually work late?" I asked.

"Most days, yes." Greyson gathered his things, turned off monitors and lights, and stowed his notebooks in drawers under the counter. I noted the various refrigerators and locked cabinets in the room, as well as a biohazard trash bin located under the counter. "I have a coworker, another researcher, who's on this project with me, but she burned her hand on a sample and had to take a leave of absence."

While he was preoccupied, I grabbed a tissue from a box on the counter, balled it up in my hand, and then stuffed it into the slot in the strike plate, my eyes on Greyson all the while.

"Yikes. How bad was it?"

"They classified it as a third-degree burn," he said, shaking his head. "We try to be careful, but accidents happen."

That was not a risk I wanted to take. Or have Sera take. Or hell, any of my brothers either.

Greyson grabbed his backpack, hefted the weight of it over his shoulder, and then turned to leave. I stepped out of the doorway as he turned off the lights and pulled the door shut behind us, testing the lever handle to make sure it was locked. I could only hope the tissue would do its job.

"Hopefully she'll be back before you know it."

"That's kind of you to say."

We passed through the facility, making it all the way to the front desk. "It was good to meet you, Greyson. I'm going to make a pit stop here." I motioned to the bathrooms. "Assuming that's okay, considering you're closing?"

He frowned, but then looked up, seeing the security guard seated behind the ticket counter, and relaxed. "Yes, you should be fine. Have a good evening."

"Same to you," I replied, ducking into the bathroom.

I waited a couple minutes before emerging. Greyson had left, but the guard was still at the desk. I walked right up to him, doing my best to look anxious.

"Everything okay?" the man asked. The logo for Solid

Security was over a silver badge on his uniform. His name tag read 'Jonesy.'

"I'm sorry to bother you, Jonesy. I must have left my jacket in the exhibits."

He frowned, pursing his lips. "You sure you brought it in with you?"

I nodded. "Definitely. It's got my car keys in it." I was mindful to be entirely honest, just in case the man had some ability to discern the truth. You could never tell, and in a town so full of supernatural beings, the risk was even higher.

"Why don't you take a quick run back through and find it? I've got to lock up, but I can give you five more minutes."

"You're a lifesaver," I replied, smiling with genuine gratitude. That was more than enough time for me to get what I needed. "I'll be quick!"

He waved at me to get moving, and I rushed back through the building, past the special supernatural only Staff Only door, and to the bench when I'd left my jacket. I threw it back on as I walked over to the lab. I pushed lightly on the door, which swung open, and then I removed the tissue from the lock mechanism, shoving it into my pocket.

I went to the refrigerator and checked the contents. There were several numbered vials, all likely logged in the system. Anything missing would raise an alarm with dear Greyson, which I definitely wanted to avoid. Plus, I couldn't steal them. I closed that door and opened the biohazard bin, eyeballing the contents. They filled the bin with vials and bags, just waiting for the cleaning crew to collect it.

Bingo! Discarded trash belonged to the dump, not the preserve. We'd be home free with these samples.

Remembering Greyson's warning about his coworker's injury, I grabbed a pair of purple latex gloves from a dispenser on the wall and slid them on. I pulled out the entire bag, carefully compressing it down. When it was flat enough, I slid it inside my jacket and zipped it up.

I had a moment of hesitation. This was my favorite jacket, made of supple, handcrafted leather, and I'd hate to damage it with pixie crap, but I didn't have anywhere else to hide the vials easily. There were a couple of petri dishes and swabs that also looked promising in the regular trash, so I snatched those as well. I closed up the bin and grabbed a spare bin liner, thinking I could use it to store the pixie poop safely for transport.

Everything tucked away in my pockets, I pulled off my gloves, stored them in my pocket to throw away later, and looked around the lab, making sure I had left nothing out of place, before I pulled the door shut behind me and made my escape, with neither Greyson nor Jonesy the wiser.

Sera

I COULDN'T STOP MYSELF FROM PACING BACK AND forth in the habitat center's small shed. A series of dim lights hung from the ceiling. Moths swirled around the lights lazily, as if they, too, were worn out by the humidity. Sweat ran down my back. It wasn't a hot day, but the area around the wetlands was unusually muggy, making it feel a good ten degrees warmer. Daylight was still dimming along the horizon, so I guessed it would be some time before the wetlands cooled off for the evening.

Even worse, wisps of mage fire continued to escape my control. I kept my arms crossed with my hands hidden up near my armpits, but I knew both of the shifters had spied my mage fire already. So far, neither had asked me about it, but it was only a matter of time.

"I thought you were the big cat?" Liam asked Marcos.

Marcos shook his head. "Yeah, even if I wanted to pace, she's taking up the only space for it in here."

Someone had conveniently left the outbuilding unlocked, and although it was pretty large, they'd packed it with excess equipment. Stacks of benches and chairs lined the room, as well as gardening equipment and tools packed on shelves that lined the walls. It was orderly enough to leave an aisle running down the middle, which was the space I'd been using to pace. Liam had taken up watch near the lone window, while Marcos stood at the door, peering out as he held it barely open.

I stopped pacing and rubbed my temples, wishing I hadn't followed Emrys and the boys through that portal. "I'm just impatient."

"I'm no longer behind this plan," Liam said, a deep

frown creasing his brow as he watched me. "We've been out here for half an hour, and I'm no good at sitting around."

"Agreed," Marcos said. "The others should be here soon. I vote we shift and go scouting for pixies to save time."

"Done," Liam replied with a decisive nod. "Our beasts will smell them out in no time."

"Didn't Greyson say shifters scared the pixies off?" I asked.

"He did, but that works for us," Marcos replied. "We don't want them, just to know where they hang out."

"Wait a sec, I don't get a vote?" I asked, planting my hands on my hips.

"In our little democracy, majority rules," Liam replied. "Unless you're in charge now?" he asked me, his playful smile daring me to challenge him.

A flicker of light flared at my fingertips, and by Liam's frown, I knew he'd seen it. Again. "No, of course not. It's just..." I stammered, hiding my hands behind my back. I needed time to manage my magic. Time with no one else watching. "On second thought, why don't you both go scout? I can wait for the others here."

"Perfect," Marcos replied, shucking off his shoes and socks.

"Will you be okay out here on your own?" Liam asked.

Whether he meant just being alone here in the shed or okay with my magic, I wasn't sure.

"I'll be fine. We're the only ones sneaking around, and I could use some time to myself," I said, hoping I projected a confidence I didn't feel. "I could use some meditation time."

Liam nodded, and then he stepped close and placed a hand on my arm, the calluses on his fingers awakening a fire beneath my skin. "I know you're a powerful mage. I won't offend you by suggesting you'd need our protection, but know we won't be far. Call out if you need anything."

Looking up into those eyes the color of emeralds, a wave of anticipation rolled over me. Momentarily tongue-tied, I nodded. The offer of protection was sweet, especially because, unlike other mages, I wasn't able to defend myself magically.

Liam moved away, taking the heat of his body with him, and I immediately felt his absence. When he joined Marcos by the door, I realized Marcos had already taken off his jacket and shirt, piling them on a shelf near the door. The dim light playing over his muscular arms and toned stomach, his skin reminding me of the shades of desert sand at dusk.

Surely that's why I was suddenly parched? Marcos wasn't as bulky as some nightclub bouncers, but I knew he could handle himself in a fight.

Liam faced away from me and pulled his shirt off over his head, his broad shoulders covered with freckled, tanned skin covered with a fine sheen of dark ginger hair. Built like a brick house and with those calloused hands, I figured he worked hard every day.

Oh, my. Things were warming up in here, and it wasn't the humidity. If I didn't know any better, I'd think they were putting on a show for me.

"Are you just going to stand there and watch us strip down?" Marcos asked, hesitating while unbuckling his belt. I knew the panther shifter was slow to warm to people. Was he also shy?

I opened my mouth to answer, but Liam beat me to the punch. "She's a lady, Marcos."

Marcos chuckled, but then looked me over. "Yeah, Sera's a lady, all right. So?"

"So... a lady does as she damn well pleases." Liam glanced at me over his shoulder, and I knew he was egging me on and giving me permission to keep watching them. He unzipped his jeans and then slid them and his underwear off at the same time.

What a flirt!

"I could use a hand fan right about now," I muttered, and they both smiled. "I didn't expect you two to strip before shifting."

"Our options are to take them off or shred them, and I'm not ruining the only clothes I have with me," Marcos replied. He turned away before dropping his pants and stepping out of them, moving as gracefully as his panther.

"I mean, I knew that. More in theory than face-to-face," I replied.

Liam turned to me and stood confidently with his shoulders back, leaving absolutely nothing to my imagination. From what I could see, which was a lot, neither Liam nor Marcos had anything to be ashamed of.

"Being naked around shifting is pretty normal in shifter culture. It's just another skin," Liam explained.

Why did I get the impression that it really mattered to him that I understood him?

"I don't think I've ever seen you shift. Or any shifter shift." I stumbled over my words, seeking something to say besides 'wow you're naked and hawt and I'm trying to keep my eyes on your face while we're talking.' "They kept us mages in our halls at the academy during those exercises."

"Sure, but have you been hiding under a rock? Supes are everywhere in our hometown," Marcos said. "There's no lack of shifters."

Heat flushed my cheeks. He'd hit on my Achilles Heel; avoiding other supes. "I haven't. My family keeps me pretty focused."

They shared a knowing look. Or was it suspicious?

I sighed. "Look, I know mages have a rep for being standoffish, but I'm not like the rest of my family."

"So we've gathered," Liam replied. "What will they think of you running off?"

I waved it off like it was nothing, but I dreaded the answer. "I doubt they'll even notice. Shouldn't you be getting going?"

"The lady's got a point," Marcos replied, running a hand through his hair.

Liam seemed to muse over something. After a moment, he shook his head, but his pensive expression remained. No doubt he'd ask me about it later.

"Let's go," he said to Marcos.

A moment later, a large white wolf with yellow eyes stood in his place. Marcos was a moment behind him, shifting into a black panther with pale leaf-green eyes. They circled me for a moment, and I had to remind myself that they weren't wild creatures. I knew them. Emboldened, I ran my fingers through their fur, and one after the other, they leaned against me, nuzzling against my hands. Marcos' purring rumbled through me, a vibration I felt in my bones.

"I didn't realize your wolf was white," I said to Liam. "I'd assumed you'd be a red wolf, cause you're a ginger."

He growl-grumbled at me.

"Okay, okay, my bad," I said. I walked over to the door, holding it open for them. "Good luck."

They shot out the door with Marcos in the lead, moving with such energy and exuberance. I wished I could run beside them. I watched them until they disappeared into the dense grasses and bushes, then closed the door.

I looked around the room before I started pacing again. Relaxing somewhat in my solitude, my mage fire reappeared, lighting up my fingertips with a flickering, eerie green glow. What could I do to fix it before they got back?

Ugh! I leaned against a stack of benches with my head in my hands and then slid down to the floor. Who was I kidding? I was stuck with these guys for the next few days. I was going to keep slipping up, and eventually they'd figure out something was wrong with my magic.

The risk wasn't just in exposing my errant magic. If I didn't get this under control, the magic would just keep leaking out. I could break something or hurt someone. I didn't have the space or time to exercise, my preferred method of burning off the magical energy.

My family was going to flip out. They'd forbidden me to associate with supes. Forbidden me from revealing my magic to others. Forbidden me from being active in magical society.

I had to do something.

I could try my energy balancing exercises. They'd never done much for me back at the academy, but maybe the little they did would be enough, until I found something else?

I crossed my legs and straightened my spine, bringing my palms together in front of me. I poured my focus into running power through my chakras. The process involved awakening each nexus, clearing any blocks, and then modulating the flow between each point.

Despite the time I put in, I made little progress. My body blocked me at every turn. There was abundant energy, but no focused outlet. No clear path through the mire of my flawed wiring. What should have worked, or at least drained some of the energy, instead stoked the hidden fires within.

Mage fire poured from my hands, surrounding my body in a bright green nimbus. The raw force of my magic raked over me like hot coals. Although I knew I could tolerate prolonged exposure, anxiety gripped at my chest. This was too much. Too fast. Too chaotic. Would I burn myself alive? The shed? The wetlands?

"Help!" I cried out, but I couldn't tell how loud I was, or if I'd even spoken out loud. Would they answer my call? Would anyone?

A MAGE ON FIRE

MARCOS

Liam and I ran for a while, his wolf side by side with my panther, enjoying the freedom of the ground under our paws and the wind in our fur. It had been so long since we'd shifted and hunted together, I'd forgotten what an easy wolf companion Liam was.

I was grateful for the time to reconnect. Since I didn't have the shifter community many others did, the few times I had with others like me were even more important to cherish.

By the time the sun had set, we'd located and sniffed out several pixie dens, but so far, none had been occupied or filled with what looked like pixie dung. We'd been traveling in a series of overlapping circles, spreading out slowly from the shed.

"How much further out do you think we should go?" I asked Liam telepathically.

He shook his head and shoulders, flinging off the dampness accumulated from thousands of wet reeds and tall grasses. *"I think we'll have to go deeper to find the pixies.*

No doubt the researchers have discouraged them from nesting too close to the habitat center. Everything we've found so far smells like they abandoned it a while ago."

He had a point. Liam always had been the reserved but clever one in our group. *"I bet Greyson and his team have cleared all the pixie dung nearby too."*

"Dung? Are you elevating our search to a scientific expedition?"

I let out a low growl, but I wasn't really sore with him. Sometimes it was just fun to flex. *"Poop sounds like something a toddler would say. So yeah, I'm gonna use other euphemisms."*

"Perhaps we should get back? The others should catch up with us soon."

I huffed. *"You know Franc and Caden will dawdle. It's good we're here to get the paw work done."*

"Well said," Liam replied. *"Still, we're not finding much to go on. Perhaps the others will have ideas that'll pan out faster."*

I turned back toward the shed, and Liam fell into step beside me. *"You're worried about Sera, aren't you?"*

"It's silly, I know. She's a powerful mage, but I can't shake this feeling that something's going on with her. Something she's not saying."

"Like you said, Liam. She's a mage. They're born harboring secrets."

That shut Liam up, and we padded along for a minute in silence.

"So then, you're not interested in Seraphina?" Liam asked, his tone nonchalant, but nonetheless it was a charged question.

"I never said that," I snapped back with more emotion than I'd intended.

A silence fell between us as we sidestepped a deeper, muddy section, giving me an opportunity to gather my thoughts. Although I loved letting my beast out to play, neither of us enjoyed trudging through sucking mud.

"Do you have any more thoughts on those marks on Sera's shoulders?" I asked, knowing he had to have been thinking it over.

Liam looked me straight in the eyes. *"You mean the mating marks."*

"Don't be cagey," I replied. *"What are we going to do? Are we supposed to fight over her?"*

"I'm sure that would give Taneisha no end of amusement to see us turn against each other, but I have no quarrel with you, brother. In fact, I've always felt we shared a special connection within our alliance because of our shared shifter heritage."

"I feel the same. So, it's bros before mages?"

If wolves could roll their eyes, I'm sure Liam would have right then. *"It's bros* and *the mage, don't you think?"*

I stopped in my tracks. The shed was in sight, but Liam and I needed to finish this conversation. *"What, you mean, we'd share Sera?"*

"Assuming she wants either of us, which is no guarantee, despite fate marking her. If she was a shifter, it might be different. We're raised with such customs. But the mage will choose whom she will."

The idea of sharing my mate rankled both my beast and me. Not that I'd even been looking for someone. Sure, my job meant I had women throwing themselves all over me nightly to get into Velvet, but I never thought of their attraction as genuine.

Sera had been strong, kind, and flirty with all of us. I didn't like how that boded for my odds at claiming her. Especially considering that I had competition.

"Sure, in the end it's up to Sera. But how are you taking this so calmly? I know how my panther feels. He wants to rush in there, pin her down, and sink his teeth into his claim."

"I'd advise against rushing a mage, especially Sera," Liam replied. *"I'm calm because I believe in love. Whatever fate has in store for me with her, I'm gonna roll with it."*

"You've changed since the academy, wolf. Back then, you were all brooding and intense. Now you're still brooding but also somehow, chill. What happened?"

"Ha. Ha. Funny kitty. A lot has happened, but that story will have to wait." Liam growled, his eyes abruptly flashing yellow and focusing on the shed.

A wave of foreboding washed over me, followed by an urge I couldn't quite name. I wanted to fight. To fuck. Maybe both. *"Something's wrong."*

We rushed back to the shed, side by side. I burst in through the door, Liam hot on my heels. Waves of mage fire whipped at my fur, the scent of my own singed fur stopping me in my tracks. We'd come face to face with Sera, sitting cross-legged on the floor, surrounded by her own mage fire.

Her expression brought fear into my heart. Panic etched Sera's features, and there was an air of desperation to her scent. Mage fire had massive destructive power, and the mage wielding it was usually immune to the effects. The floor around Sera was singed, as were the stack of benches behind her. With the amount of flame surrounding her and the blistering char of the wood, I figured we were moments away from the building catching fire.

Liam was the first to shift back, and I joined him a moment later. We kept our distance, standing just outside of the nimbus of Sera's fire. Liam handed me my pants and then pulled his jeans on while I did the same. Although we shifters are comfortable without our clothes, now was not the time for it.

"How's it going, Sera?" he asked, his voice calm, as if he was unconcerned with the popping of the wooden floorboards from the heat.

Sera held her hands in her lap, shaking her head. Beads of sweat dotted her brow, evidence of the level of mental and physical effort she was expending.

"I'm on the verge of losing control. You both need to get out of here."

"Nope, not gonna happen," I replied. "You're helping us, so the least we can do is return the favor."

"You'll get hurt if you stay. Just let me figure this out on my own."

"You won't hurt us," Liam replied, and then sat down on the floor, motioning for me to do the same. "Tell us what's happening, Sera."

She scowled, and I couldn't help but think it was the cutest thing ever, not that I'd ever tell Sera that. I wouldn't want her to stop after all.

"My powers are chaotic, pushing at the limits of my control. I did some exercises to rebalance myself and diffuse the energy, but they only made it worse."

"Could it be something Taneisha did? Some effect of

her magic on your own?" I asked. The immediate surprise in Sera's eyes told me she hadn't even considered that possibility.

"No, I don't think so. I mean it's possible, but not likely," Sera replied.

"Has this happened before with your magic?" I pressed.

"You can't tell anyone. Please guys," Sera begged. "Swear to me you won't tell anyone."

"So this has happened before." Liam nodded. "I swear I'll keep your secret," he said, and then turned to me.

Like, who was I going to tell, anyway? "I won't tell anyone. I swear it. But tell us about what's going on."

"I'm not supposed to tell anyone," she admitted, her voice a mere whisper.

Liam and I shared a look, and we didn't need words to convey our shared anger. "Says who?"

"My family." Sera sagged back against the bench. "My magic just does this. Most mages have to recharge their energy. My power just builds and builds until I discharge it."

"Is that typical for mages?" I asked. "Not to pry…"

"You're fine." She waved away my concern, an arc of green flames fanning the air with her movement. "No, it's not typical, and it's a colossal pain in the ass."

"Which is why your family makes you keep it a secret?" Liam asked. "Because they don't want anyone to know your magic is different?"

Sera rolled her eyes. "Yes. They're ashamed of me, but mostly they don't want the family's reputation for magical prowess diminished. It's why I live on my own, separate from supe society."

"Yikes." I shook my head. "I thought being away from my shifter family was bad. At least they didn't reject me," I replied. "So, if you discharge the energy, you'll regain control over the mage fire?"

Sera nodded. "That's why I'm trying to let it just burn off. It always works. But it's not working now."

"I'd bet you can thank our trickster fae for that," Liam growled out.

Sera looked back and forth between the two of us, seeking confirmation. I nodded my agreement. "Taneisha may not have caused the problem, but I wouldn't put it past her to turn our weaknesses against us to prevent us from winning her challenges."

"I hadn't thought of that, but you're right. I wouldn't put it past her either," Sera replied.

"What do you normally do to regain balance?" Liam asked.

"Exercise, mostly. Cardio. Lots of cardio. But I can't do that like this." She held up her hands.

"I could really go for some cardio myself," I said to Liam.

"That mage fire might slow you down, tiger," he replied.

She needed to burn off mental and physical energy fast. *"There's more than one way to make a cup of coffee. I have an idea. Follow my lead?"*

He arched his brow but gave me a quick nod.

"I just want to point out you could have asked us for help, you know? It's ironic that you've been giving the posse hell for not working together or asking for help. You haven't been following your own advice."

Sera laughed, and the flames grew for a moment. Had I made the fire worse? But no, another couple of seconds passed, during which the fire seemed to get a little smaller.

Liam glanced at me, giving me a quick nod, and I knew he'd seen it too.

"I suppose you're right," Sera said. "But now you know my secret."

"That you're an amazingly potent mage?" Liam said, his voice teasing. "I'm afraid we've known that since our academy days, darling."

Sera blinked slowly, a smile playing across her face, warring with confusion. She let out a halfhearted laugh; the fire blazing with her emotions. "You know that's not what I meant. I meant that my magic is chaotic."

"All supes have their own trials and tribulations. It's the burden we have to bear for being extraordinary," I said.

This time Sera's laugh was full-throated, and her smile took my breath away. I sucked in a sigh of relief when her mage fire retreated another few inches.

"Good instincts," Liam said to me. *"The fire has diminished."*

"I'd still prefer a more full-contact method, but glad this seems to help."

Caught in a laughing fit, Sera brought her hands up to her head. "This is so ridiculous." Racked by laughter, she leaned forward, gasping out phrases one by one. "I've been sucked through Faery. Stuck with the five hottest guys from school. Hunting pixie poop. Setting a shed on fire. Revealing my deep dark secret."

"Wait, wait, the hottest guys from academy?" I asked, shocked by her admission. "You mean us?"

She glanced up at me, tears of amusement rolling down her cheeks. "Duh. Have you even looked at yourselves?" Sera waved at us.

Liam and I hadn't taken the time to put on anything

but our pants. Now we sat here, shirtless and sweating from the heat of her remaining mage fire.

"I mean, you're a curious bunch, but damn. I'd actually wondered if you'd all made friends just to segregate the academy's hotness into the most compact space possible and lord it over the rest of us. Like a supernova of hotness."

Sera succumbed to another laughing fit, which was good, cause I needed a moment to pick my jaw up off the floor.

"Wow," Liam replied, chuckling. "Let me assure you, that was not deliberate. But why a supernova?"

Sera finished laughing and then shrugged. "Because you were untouchable. Out of reach."

"Pshaw," Liam replied, and I knew my expression had to match the incredulity on his. "You could have crooked your finger and had any of us, Sera."

Sera bit her lip. "Even if I had realized that then, I was too anxious to make a move."

The green flames had mostly dissipated, visible only at her fingertips. Relief washed over me, not only that the crisis had been averted, but also that Liam and I had been there to help Sera thought it.

"Looks like your mage fire is back under control. What about now?" I asked, daring her to answer. To be bold.

It was Sera's turn to gape at me. She checked her hands and realized the flames had gone out. Sera shot to her feet and broke into a dance, wiggling her hips and rocking out. "It's gone. I can't believe it. You both talked me down."

Liam and I stood. I couldn't stop smiling at the giddy look of joy on Sera's face or tear my gaze away from the way she swayed her body to her own rhythm.

"I prefer Supernova of Hotness over posse, what do you think?" Liam asked me, carrying on the conversation as if I hadn't just invited Sera into something more intimate.

"I guess Supernova of Hotness is our new posse name. The others will have to deal," I said.

Sera threw her arms around Liam, her curvy body colliding with his. "Thank you," she said, her voice raspy.

Liam's arms wrapped around Sera, his hands gripping around her waist and shoulders, burying his nose in her raven hair. When he looked up at me, his eyes flashed yellow as his wolf neared the surface. I didn't think of myself as the jealous type, but at that moment, I wanted to rip her out of his arms, strip her naked, and cover Sera with my scent.

Sera relaxed against Liam, and when she pulled away, there was a moment where she paused and they locked gazes. I wondered if they'd kiss. Then Sera pulled away from him and turned to me, wrapping her arms around my shoulders and leaning her face against my neck.

"Thank you too," she whispered.

With the heat of her body pressing against mine, I got instantly hard. My panther clawed at the surface, straining to claim our mage. My hands ran down Sera's sides, and she shivered under my touch. I gently grazed my fingertips from her hips up along her spine to her shoulder blades, drawing a gasp from her full lips. Sera arched her back, pulling away slightly until her lips brushed against the side of my face.

I waited for Sera to make her move, my body tense and ready to pounce. My energy coiled tight as a spring, hanging on her every movement. Something flashed in her eyes. A moment of unsure vulnerability followed by raw determination.

I got little time to wonder about it, because Sera slid her palm around the back of my neck and pulled me down, planting those luscious lips of hers against mine. My mind blanked out for a moment in shock.

Was this really happening?

My panther urged me on, and a moment later I had Sera pinned up against a shelf, my mouth on hers as I explored her glorious curves with my hands. Her scent drove me wild, reminding me of honeysuckle blossoms on a hot, sunny afternoon. I ravished her neck with a line of kisses, nibbling as I went, spurred on by her gasps and moans.

Sera's fingers dug into my hips, gripping me against her. "I want you," she whispered, and I looked up into her eyes, seeing the desire within. "Both of you." Sera looked up over my shoulder at Liam, biting her lip. "Also, this shelf isn't working for me."

"Give me a moment," Liam replied.

"If both of us are what you want, that's what you'll get," I replied, my voice low. I heard Liam moving things around behind us in the shed as I lingered, tracing the outline of a nipple through Sera's t-shirt. She arched against me, grinding her hips against my cock, and I let out a groan. "It seems like this sort of works for you."

Sera's wicked little smile was all I needed, at least until she wrapped her arms around my neck, kissing me again with abandon, further fueling the fire between us. I pulled her away from the shelf, wrapped my arms around her, and then lifted her up. She wrapped her legs around my hips, and I carried her over to the bench Liam had freed up along the wall. He'd thrown our jackets down, covering the wooden surface.

Liam came up behind Sera, sandwiching her between our bodies. "All you had to do was ask, little mage," Liam growled out against her neck.

She threw back her head, seeking a kiss that Liam was all too eager to deliver. While they were occupied, I unzipped Sera's jeans and then got on my knees before her. After I helped her out of her shoes and socks, I peeled her pants down and off her legs. Her undies were the same bubblegum pink as her shirt, with the phrase '+3 Potion of Heroism' emblazoned in red ink.

I chuckled, tracing the letters, and Sera squirmed under my touch. "Why heroism?"

Sera pulled away from her kiss with Liam, looking down to see what I meant. "Oh, that?" She arched her brow. "Because going down is what heroes do."

"Then it looks like I'm the hero you need," I said, hooking my fingers through the waistband and rolling them down over her hips. I didn't hesitate. I dove right in, eager to worship at the altar nestled between her thighs. Liam held Sera against him, bearing her weight as I lifted her left foot onto my shoulder, gripping the globes of her ass in my hands.

The scent of her pussy drove me mad with hunger for her, and I swear I could have licked and flicked my tongue against her wet folds for hours. Sera ground her pelvis against my mouth, moaning low in her throat as Liam cupped her breasts in his hands under her shirt. Every time she cried out, I redoubled my efforts.

If she couldn't walk later, I'd take full responsibility.

The mage fire blossomed in her hands again, and I

wondered for a moment if the situation could turn dangerous. But I trusted Sera, even knowing her powers were chaotic, to tell us if she needed to stop.

"Oh, oh, yes!" Sera cried out, arching against us both, her body a live wire conducting electricity. A wave of charged heat rolled off her flesh, reminding me of touching metal that had been sitting in the sun all afternoon, but that sensation passed quickly.

Sera caught her breath for a moment while I kissed my way up her thighs and belly. I pulled the hem of her shirt up and over her head, revealing the hot pink satin bra hidden underneath. Her breasts were full, almost too full for the satin bra. Liam managed the clasp, his lips tracing a path to her shoulders, when he slipped the straps off and then tossed the bra over to join her other clothes.

For a few moments we explored her body together, nibbling, kissing, and sucking our way over the canvas of her exposed flesh.

"You guys are wearing way too much, and it's about to get a lot hotter in here." That was all she had to say for Liam and me to take our pants off. While we were busy, Sera pulled away and opened the window over the bench Liam had prepped. When she turned back around, Sera's gaze swept over each of us.

I didn't think it was possible to get any harder than I was, but the way Sera looked at us was so hungry. So feral. I almost came on the spot.

She crooked one index finger at me and one at Liam. Actually crooked them at us! I couldn't help but laugh.

Liam shook his head. "I'm not about to turn down that invitation."

Sera reached out and pulled us with her to the bench.

She looked like a woman with a plan, so I let her steer me to one end of the bench. "I want you to sit," she said, so I did. Sera got onto all fours in front of me, pulling Liam by the hand behind her.

Liam searched through his jacket, producing a condom. Supes were immune to human diseases, but not to pregnancy. Sera nodded up at him as he rolled it onto his shaft.

I normally preferred being in charge, but having our curvy mage direct the action was such a turn-on, I wasn't about to argue. I stroked my cock, drawing Sera's attention right where I wanted it.

"I love a woman who knows what she wants."

When she leaned forward and took me in her mouth, I sucked in a sharp breath.

I ran my hands through Sera's hair, appreciating her efforts, as I watched her reach back, take Liam's shaft in her hand, and position him between her legs.

"Happy to oblige, little mage," Liam said.

Liam's look of near reverence as he moved into Sera made me almost regret our positions, but her renewed enthusiasm changed my mind quick enough. I grasped a handful of her raven hair at her nape, encouraging her pacing.

That's when I got a better look at the marks on her shoulders in the dim light. I froze for a moment in confusion, and Sera stopped and looked up at me.

"Everything okay?" she asked, her brows knit with a little frown.

I wanted to say, how can they not be with your hand gripping my cock like you own it, but thought better of it.

"I can't imagine being more okay. You're amazing Sera," I answered.

Sera smiled that sultry smile of hers, and then her lips were back, sliding down my shaft. I almost forgot what I'd seen under her blissful attention.

"What do you think of the markings?" Liam asked me telepathically. His hands gripped Sera's hips, and I felt every thrust of his as I pumped into her mouth.

I was right at the edge, but his question made me focus. *"I see a wolf's moon. A panther's paw print. Something like an ankh? A grape leaf. And some sort of sigil?"*

"The moon and paw are classic mate markings." His gaze met mine. *"She's our mate."*

My hold on the conversation was failing, distracted by the orgasm Sera was eager to pull out of me. *"But not just ours. There are three other marks."*

A moment hung in the air, and I knew we were both thinking the same thing. There were five marks. Five in our Supernova of Hotness posse.

I growled, my panther eager to claim Sera as my own. My willingness to share with Liam was one thing. *"The entire posse? No way,"* I said. Liam and I had dated women together before, so that wasn't entirely new territory. *"She's ours."*

But Caden? Never. Franc? Maybe. Emrys? Nowadays he grated on my nerves after a single evening.

"This is very unusual. I've never heard of non-shifters having mate markings. It must be an effect of the fae magic."

Liam rocked Sera forward, driving deep into her and forcing my cock deep into her throat. I couldn't last any longer, crying out as I shot into her throat.

"Hey, is everything okay in there?" came Franc's voice through the open window.

"We heard something and came running," Caden said.

Liam and I froze while Sera continued to squirm against Liam. Then she surprised me yet again.

"We're fine, guys. Door's around the other side. Come on in," Sera said, a bit of a sparkle in her eyes as she called out the window.

I might be comfortable in all of my skins, but I certainly wasn't the exhibitionist Sera just revealed herself to be. I tried to scramble, to move out from underneath her, but Sera planted her hands on my thighs, resting her head against my stomach.

"Don't you dare stop, Liam," she ordered.

Liam

I WASN'T ABOUT TO REFUSE A LADY, ESPECIALLY ONE I knew was my mate. I soldiered on, balls deep in Sera, as the shed door swung open.

Marcos, who just a minute ago looked to have been having the best orgasm of his life, now looked fit to bolt.

Franc sauntered in like a king who owned the place, arching his brow as he took in the three of us. Caden slipped in behind him, shut the door, and then came to a dead halt when he saw us. There was an instant fiery satisfaction in his eyes as he fed off the sexual energy in the room.

"This is not the pixie hunt I expected," Franc said. "But I'm here for it."

"I'm just disappointed we didn't start it," Caden added. "Can we stay?"

"Uh-huh," Sera said. "I want you to watch."

I continued my thrusts, and Sera kept grinding against me. By the way her sheath contracted around me, and her whimpers and quickened breath, I knew she was loving every minute of this.

Caden let out a low moan, and I glanced up to see Franc in front of him, unzipping his pants, and enthusiastically taking his sizable erection between his lips. Based on their unspoken familiarity, clearly this was not a new behavior between them. No wonder Franc hadn't excluded Caden from his club, despite the allegations of his drug use and meeting unsavory characters within it.

Sera watched the incubus and demigod, the action revving up her movements. So our Sera wasn't just an exhibitionist, but a voyeur as well. Marcos' expression flipped back and forth between being mortified by Franc and Caden watching us, and enraptured by Sera writhing in front of him, impaled on my cock.

"Relax and roll with it," I told him. *"And play with her nipples."*

Marcos appeared to shake off his discomfort by refocusing on Sera. She sighed at his touch, seeming to blossom under all our focused attention.

Despite the interruptions and company, I was still hard. No, that wasn't true. I knew full well why I didn't falter. Sera was my mate, our mate, and I was the first to have her. If I had my way, I'd be the first to claim her too.

I was getting ahead of myself, but imagining claiming Sera, sealing her future with mine, had me increasing my pace and nearing my release. I reached around her hips, sliding my fingers into her folds, circling her clit with my fingertips.

I let myself fully focus on Sera, feeling my peak coming hard and fast, and needing to see Sera reach hers first. I heard Caden let out a yell. Despite the effects of his muting necklace, a wave of pleasure rolled off him, hitting all of us. A moment later, Sera's spine arched and her breath hitched, her inner walls fluttering and then clamping down, milking the orgasm out of me. The pleasure was so great; I heard my yell erupt from my lips as if from a disembodied distance.

I sat back, and Sera collapsed, half in my lap, half splayed across Marcos' legs. Marcos was threading his fingers through her hair, petting her as his gaze remained on the mate markings along her shoulders.

"That was mind-blowing," Sera murmured.

"Not what I'd expected," Marcos replied. "But I'm sure glad it happened."

The door to the shed flew open, and it was a measure of our spent energy that none of us jumped up in reaction. Emrys rushed in, a look of panic on his face.

"What's wrong?" he gasped out, stopping before he ran into Franc, who was rising to his feet as Caden zipped up his pants around his still-hard—or was it growing again?—erection. No doubt for the incubus, that blowjob was only a taster for the depths of his sexual appetite.

As Emrys took in the room, his expression transformed from a look of concern, through a pained look of betrayal, to a flash of anger as his cheeks flushed. Only then did I recall he wasn't with us. If I'd been in his shoes, I'd have felt left out too.

"What the hell, guys?"

WAIT... FATED WHAT'S?
SERA

I didn't realize Emrys had arrived until I heard his words and the accusation in his tone. I opened my eyes, my mind still hazy from the bliss of multiple orgasms and the discharge of my magic. And what a way to do it!

Normally, I would have been too shy to even think of burning my magical overload off with sex. I'd stuck to marathon gym sessions because of their simplicity and availability. But this forced proximity with the posse gave me an opportunity to explore new avenues. Best of all: we were only together for the time needed to complete the fae's tasks. When all of this was over, we'd go our separate ways with some delicious memories. No one had to be the wiser.

I felt bad Emrys had missed the action. But there was time for that later, right? Oh my gods, my brain had gone all sex-addled. But hell, I was having a hard time coming up with reasons that might be a bad thing.

Emrys stood in the middle of the room, holding what

looked like a red plastic bag in one hand. "I'm gone for an hour, and I come back to an orgy?" he asked. "Why aren't you out looking for pixies?"

"We did that, but when we couldn't find anything, Marcos and I came back here to wait for you guys to catch up with us," Liam explained.

"Doesn't seem like you waited very long," he spat out.

"Caden and I arrived a few minutes ago ourselves," Franc added. "Still plenty of time for us to join in for the crescendo."

"At least in part," Caden murmured, wiggling his brows at Franc.

I thought back through watching Franc giving Caden the blowjob, the thrill of the memory causing a belated shiver of pleasure to run through me. It hadn't appeared to be the first time for either of them, as they'd moved with an ease and familiarity reserved for lovers.

I wouldn't mind watching that again. But then my gaze fell on Emrys, who couldn't take his eyes off the pile of me, Liam, and Marcos. His intensity bored through me, a possessive edge to his energy. Suddenly, I felt overly aware of having everyone's eyes on my naked self.

"Where have you been?" Liam asked.

I pushed myself up to standing, accepting an overabundance of help from both Marcos and Liam, intent on getting my clothes back on as quickly as I could.

"I've been salvaging pixie poop from the trash," Emrys said and then pointed at Marcos. "For you."

"You found some?" I asked, pulling my underwear back on. Marcos held my bra up for me, and I turned my back to the door and the others while I put it on. "That's fantastic."

"I did, but then I walked into this," Emrys said. "It's like you guys aren't taking this situation seriously. We're here to get our treasures back, not get distracted wasting time with orgies in sheds."

"I can assure you, we didn't waste a single moment," Liam responded, buttoning up his jeans. He grabbed mine off the floor and handed them to me. "We might as well enjoy ourselves along the way, right?"

I swear there could have been steam pouring out of Emrys' ears. Franc held up a hand, causing Emrys to hold back what would have been a snappy reply. "There's a better question you should take seriously, Em. Just how many mate markings are there on Seraphina's shoulders?"

With one leg of my jeans on and the other halfway there, my heart skipped a beat. "What did you say?" I whipped around, losing my balance as I went.

Luckily, Franc and Emrys caught me, preventing my fall. Wedged between the two of them, Franc's words momentarily fled my mind. But then Emrys pulled my hair to the side, getting a good look at my back and shoulders.

"What do you see?" I asked, pulling my jeans up and zipping them.

"It's... not possible," Emrys stammered, his expression a mix of denial and confusion. "That's just ridiculous. A fae trick, here to distract us from our quest."

"What's on my back?" I demanded, looking each of them in the eye, one by one, but none of them appeared eager to answer.

When my gaze fell on Liam, he didn't look away. "There are mate markings. Five in total. I assume they weren't there before you crossed over into Faery with us?"

"Five?" I asked. Liam and the others nodded. "Of course they weren't there before. And you'd seen them before we just..." my voice trailed off.

"Marcos and I both did," Liam replied, not shying away from the truth. "Although our beasts both felt the call to claim you before we saw the marks."

Liam held out my t-shirt to me, which I snatched from his hand, and then pulled over my head.

"Claim me? Like a piece of property?" Who did they think I was? I mean, they were the Supernova of Hotness, but still. How dare fate stick me in this situation? "Fated mates? Just because we have a fun romp doesn't mean any of you," I pointed at each of them, "get to 'claim' me. Got it?"

"Of course not, Sera," Marcos replied, rubbing the back of his neck. "None of us would do anything against your will. You're not obligated or being forced into anything. It's all your choice."

It relieved me to hear Marcos say it, but the mere existence of mate markings on me felt like fate had dropped a hammer. My life wasn't perfect, but I liked it how it was. Didn't I? I had enough to deal with managing my family, my mundane job, and my chaotic magic.

"They've got to be a fae trick to mess with our minds and put us off our game. Demigods and demons don't have mate markings," Emrys scoffed. "Don't worry, Sera, fate isn't bossing either of us around."

I wanted to believe Emrys' bravado, but if he was wrong, where did that leave me? I'd assumed this was a brief adventure, a foray into the supe society that I had to abandon years ago, followed by a return to my normal life in the shadows. If fate was lining me up with a mate, even multiple mates, I didn't even know what to do with that.

"The fae can't trick fate," Liam replied. "Perhaps, because shifters are involved, the other mate markings showed up as well?"

"I know we're feeling all the feels here," Franc said. "Might I suggest we take the pixie poop Emrys saved from the trash back to Amber and get these trades unwinding? Perhaps the walk with help us all process and clear our minds a little."

"It's the middle of the night," I said.

"Amber said she'd wait up for us to return," Marcos replied.

"Fine," I said, pushing past them out of the door. I didn't want to talk to any of them right now.

A CRAP TRADE

MARCOS

"This isn't quite what I expected," Amber said, looking over the pile of yellow-tinged cotton swabs stuffed into the biohazard bag.

I'd insisted that everyone stay outside, and most of them had listened to me. All but Emrys, of course. No one could tell him what to do.

"You didn't specify how you wanted the pixie poop delivered, so we worked with what we had available," Emrys said. He leaned against the counter, flashing Amber that blatantly sexy smile of his.

Amber didn't strike me as the type of woman one could charm with a pretty face. Gratefully, we had what she wanted, so guile wasn't required.

"I'll make a note to be more specific in the future. However," she continued, "it's more than enough to meet the terms of our arrangement."

Emrys turned back to the rest of us, dripping with smug confidence. "Good thing not all of us were distracted, eh?"

Sera, who stood with her arms crossed, rolled her eyes at him. I loved that she was taking none of his shit.

Amber set the bag down on her desk, walked over to a potting bench, and returned with a small Altruscan Orchid in a pot the size of my hand. There was a stem with buds running along it, but none of the small golden flowers had opened yet.

I took the pot and sighed with relief. I was one step closer to getting my panther icon back.

"Any special directions for its care?"

She pursed her lips. "Jasper should know what to do. If he doesn't, tell him he can come see me and I'll walk him through it."

I chuckled. "Let me guess. For a price?"

Amber shrugged. "Girl's got to make a living."

"Thank you," I said. "This means the world to me."

"Thanks for your business," she called over her shoulder. "I trust you can show yourselves out?"

Twenty minutes later, we were back at the bowling alley. Lit up with bright neon, black lights, and blaring disco music, the aged space was trying a bit too hard to invoke funky town.

This time, I alone stood across from Jasper, the owner. He sat behind the counter, playing a cross between DJ and league commentator on the microphone. He downed the last of his mug as we rolled up. Jasper locked eyes on me like a homing missile, a smile spreading across his face.

I carried the Altruscan Orchid up to Jasper, glad we were one step closer to wrapping this up.

"You can drink coffee at this hour?" I asked, placing the plant on the counter in front of him.

He chuckled ruefully. "Chamomile tea, if you must know."

I laughed. "I suppose that makes a bit more sense."

"I see you've wheedled an orchid out of Amber's grasp for me?" he asked, and I nodded. "I'm not sure how you managed it, but I'm grateful." He inspected the small plant, no larger than his fist. "I'd hoped for some blooms on the orchid."

"Amber said she could help you with that?"

"Hah. I'm sure she can." He turned around and opened the case containing the Eye of the Tiger, handling it gingerly. "Be careful with this."

I accepted it, cradling it between my palms. The orb hummed, and I felt it vibrating all the way into my bones. "Is it supposed to do that?"

He frowned. "Yup. I hope it's all you imagined."

I wasn't after the orb for its divinatory properties, just as a means to an end, so I had little expectation. Just for the Eye to satisfy Taneisha's demands.

"I'm sure it will. Thank you, Jasper. Fair trade?"

"Fair trade, young man. Now be on your way."

I was eager to get on my way and back to the posse. Or as Sera had renamed us, the Supernova of Hotness.

Which may have been the tamest part of today so far. I laughed to myself.

But when I rejoined everyone outdoors, the stress in the air was palpable. "Everything okay?"

"Did you get the Eye?" Sera asked.

"I did. You guys seem tense?" I asked.

Caden huffed. "Beyond the obvious awkwardness, there was a patrol car rolling by earlier. We're a bunch of tourists and I don't get the impression the locals like us wandering around late at night."

I nodded. "Fair enough. Let's call Taneisha and get this wrapped up."

Sera held up her hand. "Hold on, she'd said to invoke her from a secluded location. I think we should get off the main drag first, in case someone is watching."

Franc pointed across and down the street. "There's an alley leading to a parking lot behind the bar."

There were nods, and then Franc led the way.

I carried the Eye close to my chest, almost like a football. The humming kept shifting, which I assumed was normal. I suppose I should have asked more about it, but it's not like I'd be using it. The relic was for Taneisha, not us.

"Not everything is relative to a bar," Liam rumbled.

"You wound me, my friend," Franc replied, hand held over his heart. "Bars aren't just places to drink. They're for gathering with friends. Telling our stories around the proverbial fire. Building community. Dancing ourselves into ecstatic states. Transcending our humdrum lives."

"Clever speech," Sera said. "But I don't get the impression you're having any difficulty enjoying your life."

Shifting its pattern, the Eye began thrumming in cycles of three. Anxiety washed over me, but I wasn't sure what to do about it.

"What can I say?" Franc said, a wicked glint in his eyes. "I'm a professional."

"Which is exactly what I'd expect the god of wine and drama to say," Liam replied.

Franc smiled, but there was a tension in his shoulders

that wasn't there a moment ago. "Theater, Liam. Drama is for queens."

We turned the corner into the alley, but per our luck, the parking lot wasn't empty, despite the late hour. We stopped short. It was immediately obvious this wasn't the spot we were looking for.

Franc checked his watch. "Damn, it's past one. I bet they're past their last call, so the patrons are heading out."

"Good call on our portal location," Sera said, smacking Franc on the shoulder. "Here I thought you were the expert on bars."

"Let's just turn around and find the next alley," Emrys said.

"Hey, that's the guy!" said a man in the parking lot. A guy who, to my keen panther ears, sounded a lot like the habitat tech, Greyson.

Crap. That didn't bode well. Neither did the faster vibrations coming from the Eye.

It was only then that I realized one of the vehicles was a police car.

Greyson led a handful of men across the parking lot toward us while Emrys turned and headed back toward the street. Franc and Caden followed the demigod. Sera hesitated.

"Hey," Greyson said. "Stop! I need to talk to you."

Emrys just kept on walking. That's when I knew he was guilty of something.

Sera moved in close to me, Liam by her side. "We really should have asked how Em got the pixie trash," she whispered.

"We were distracted," Liam said under his breath.

"Come on, guys," Emrys called back to us.

"I'm not running from a talk," Sera said. "And not the local law. Not in a town full of supes. Do not escalate things."

My stomach sank. She was right. We had the out to Faery, but we couldn't do that with others present. "Hell," I whispered. "Get back here," I called to Emrys.

Sera didn't budge, so Liam and I didn't either. Franc and Caden stood behind us while Emrys slowly trudged his way back.

We didn't get to talk more because Greyson, a cop, and a few of their friends had caught up with us. I glanced at Liam, knowing I didn't need to tell him that all of them were wolf shifters.

A fuming Greyson reached us a few seconds later. "You've stolen from me."

"Stolen what?" I asked, a sinking feeling in the pit of my stomach. I gripped the Eye close to my side, fearing all the running around tonight wouldn't be enough to get my icon back.

"You know what!" he yelled. "The cleaning crew alerted the night guard, and they just called me. Said someone took my trash out, only I didn't do it. Jonesy said a swanky city boy had gone back into the back. I know it was you," he said, pointing at Emrys.

"I'm Officer Bouchard. Is that true?" said the lady wolf shifter with the badge.

Emrys put on his charm, full of smiles for the woman, which she ignored. "Okay, yes, officer, like Jonesy said, I went back and got my jacket, which I'd left. On my way out I took the trash with me, as a favor."

"What's your name?" she asked him.

He hesitated a moment. Our names had power, even more so the names of demigods. "Emrys Tedros."

"You stole my trash!" Greyson accused.

Emrys held his hand to his chest. "Okay, I get you're not grateful for my help, but I wasn't aware a person could steal trash? I mean, you'd already thrown it out."

"Trash is the property of the owner until it's removed from the property," Bouchard replied. "Where's it at now?"

"We don't have it. I disposed of it in the dumpster, of course," Emrys said.

We all knew it was a lie, but no one argued about it.

Greyson huffed. "The cleaning crew looked in the dumpster and said it wasn't there. Besides, to get that trash, you'd have to break into my office to get it."

Emrys played it off, shrugging his shoulders and holding up his hands like he was confused. If I didn't know better, I might have believed him myself. "The door was open when I got there."

"Nonsense! You were with me when I shut it." Greyson turned to Bouchard. "You should bring these criminals in for questioning."

"You can search us," I offered. Sera nodded at me in encouragement. "See for yourselves, we don't have your trash."

"I'll take you up on that offer," Bouchard replied. "Open your jackets and bags." Bouchard did the rounds, checking Emrys first and then the others. Last, she walked right up to me. I held open my jacket, which she did a cursory glance over. It's not like I could hide a bag of biohazard trash anywhere. "What exactly are you doing with Jasper's Eye?"

"It's our reason for coming into town. We bought it off him for a friend," I replied.

Bouchard let out a low whistle. Tension in the alley had ratcheted up a few notches. I wasn't sure if she was inclined to believe me or not.

"See, they're career criminals! I knew it! Jasper would never sell that Eye!" Greyson said.

"Cool your jets, Greyson. I'm gonna give old Jasper a call and check out this kid's story. What's your name?"

"Marcos Wright."

"Hold on. Nobody goes anywhere." She pulled out a phone and made a call. "Hey Jasper..." she started, but my focus on her words faded as a half dozen wolf shifters entering the alley behind us, walking on padded feet, hackles raised.

"You're not going anywhere," Greyson declared.

"We weren't leaving," Sera replied, addressing the newcomer wolves.

They'd penned us in. In front of us we had the parking lot with Greyson, his friends, and Officer Bouchard. From behind in the alley, we had the wolves, who were growling and pacing.

Sera's hands sparked up with the green glow of her mage fire, illuminating the brick walls of the surrounding alleyway. The wolves keened and backed off a few paces but didn't leave. Her fire sputtered and flared, and then fizzled out. I wondered, if pressed, what magic Sera could muster in this moment.

But that was a topic for another time. Right now, we just needed to de-escalate things.

"Everyone, just keep your cool," I said under my breath like a prayer.

Officer Bouchard got off the phone, tucking it into her jacket, shaking her head. "That was Jasper. He said you paid for the Eye," she said to me.

"We did, ma'am."

"Well then, that settles that part. Greyson," Bouchard said, "I'm not finding your trash on them now. Can you prove they broke into your office?"

Greyson planted his hands on his hips. "No. Jonesy found it locked, and the lock wasn't damaged."

"What harm are you claiming this Emrys fellow caused?" Officer Bouchard asked.

"He took my trash, which was full of remnants of pixie dung!" he said, as if that should explain everything.

"Which, if true, they don't have any now," Officer Bouchard said. "What's the worry about some lost poop, anyway?"

Greyson's exasperation was cute, but he'd run out of rope with the officer. "It's dangerous! Explosive in high enough quantities. You can hurt yourself with it."

"Dangerous, huh? Is it illegal to have it without a license?" she asked.

"In large enough quantities, yes," he said. "It's that risky."

"Did you have that much in your trash?" Officer Bouchard asked.

"Well, no," Greyson admitted.

Bouchard sighed the sigh of the perpetually overworked and exasperated. "Then there's nothing provable to charge them with, Greyson. I recommend everyone go home and get some rest. Now."

Greyson huffed but turned and stalked off toward the cars. "This is not over," he called over his shoulder. His bar friends wandered off with him, and the wolves skulked off behind us.

Officer Bouchard turned to me. "That goes for you too."

"Officer, I want to assure you we're leaving town right now. We're not planning to return either," I said.

Officer Bouchard held my gaze, and then nodded, satisfied with my claim. "That's good to hear. Safe travels."

As the officer walked off, we all held our breath for a collective moment. When it passed, of course, Emrys was the first with a pithy comeback.

"That was close," Emrys said. "Good thing we could talk some sense into the officer."

Sera stomped up to Emrys. "That was only close because of you. What the hell were you thinking?"

Emrys clenched his jaw, and I moved in, intent to keep them from fighting. Not just because we needed to get out of here in case the pack returned. Emrys and Sera were mates, whether or not either of them wanted that to be the case. The last thing any of us needed was added strife in that already tenuous connection.

A connection we all now shared, and I was all too aware that we were nowhere near sealing our bonds together.

Emrys leaned close to Sera. "I was thinking we needed to get back Marcos' icon. What were you thinking about back in that shed? Marcos' legacy?"

"That's uncalled for, Em. I know tempers are high, but can we talk this out later?" I asked.

The fire in Sera's eyes tempered, and she took a couple of steps back from Emrys. "Fine. Are we alone enough to say the magic words?"

I rolled the Eye of the Tiger orb between my hands. We needed to act before anyone else showed up. I motioned to the others. "Gather round." When they came close, I spoke. "Taneisha. Taneisha. Taneisha."

A moment later a whirlwind formed around our feet, building momentum until it swept up and over us, transporting us back to Faery on swirling wisps of rainbow-colored sparkles.

EPILOGUE - TRUTH AND CONSEQUENCES

SERA

The magical teleportation back to Faery should have been a wondrous feat. Yet another thing I wouldn't get to see in my supe-free day-to-day life, but all I could think about was how frustrated I was at Emrys. Taneisha had warned us all not to cheat, not to steal, but that's exactly what he had done.

Perhaps she hadn't noticed, but I doubted we were that lucky.

The rainbow sparkles from the whirlwind slowed their pace, moving erratically about now that they'd been freed from the sucking vortex of the portal. Seconds later, they transformed into lightning bugs in an enchanting array of jewel tones. When the surrounding air cleared, we were back in Taneisha's forest glen, but, mirroring the mundane world, it was also now nighttime.

Central in the grove, Taneisha reclined on a chaise lounge atop a dais made of hewn granite. She looked like she'd been resting for some time in her private grotto, but I suspected she'd posed for dramatic effect during our arrival.

"That was quick," Taneisha said, rising to her feet. She wore a full-length, off the shoulder dress made of what looked to be deep crimson rose petals.

Was it just an enchantment? A fabric made to look like roses? I couldn't tell. Perhaps if I had better control of my magic, but that fate wasn't in my cards.

"I trust you were successful in attaining the Eye of the Tiger for me?" she asked.

"We have it," Marcos replied, holding it up to show her. When she beckoned Marcos forward, he walked it up to her, depositing the globe in her outstretched hands.

"Oh, my lovely darling, how I've waited for you," Taneisha murmured to the orb.

I wanted to leave Taneisha alone with her pretty bauble, cause it seemed like they needed a moment. But where could we go? She had in us a captive audience.

When she looked back up at us, as if remembering we were still here in her private space, Taneisha slid the orb into a pocket on her skirt, which somehow easily fit the orb.

"I am so jealous." The words had just slipped out before I could censor myself.

But, by her genuine smile, Taneisha didn't seem to mind. "I know, right? I'll get you the name of my tailor. Proper pockets, every time."

"Those are more like bags of holding," I said. When she frowned, I explained. "It's a magical item that's bigger on the inside."

"Yes, that's exactly what he does," she said, beaming. Taneisha dipped her hand into another pocket of her skirt, pulling out a soapstone black panther out of her pocket, holding it out for Marcos.

He held out his hand, but she hesitated. "Say you're sorry."

His jaw ticked, but Marcos' focus was absolute. "I'm sorry I was an ass to you at the academy. I ignored you and I was rude. I apologize."

Taneisha's face lit up, and she dropped the icon into Marcos' hand. "See, that wasn't that hard. I accept your apology, and from now forward, there will be no ill will between us."

Marcos wrapped his hand around the item and then slid it into his jacket pocket. "Agreed."

I let out a breath of tension I hadn't realized I'd been holding. Hopefully, things would go as smoothly as they could, with no mention of Emrys' questionable behavior.

"Now that we've taken care of that, let me tell you about your next quest." Taneisha crossed the glen to a large oak tree and knocked on it like one might a door. A moment later, the bark swung inwards, revealing the outline of the trunk as a door frame, the other side a place not Faery, but a hilly land coated in moonlight.

"Through this portal you will seek Caden's jar of seeds atop the mountain." She pointed, and we could just make out the tallest spire in the moonlight.

I looked at her. "Wait, I thought you were holding all of their items?"

Taneisha shrugged and hummed. "That was my plan, but while you were away, I was attacked. Can you believe it? They stole Caden's item from me. Me! Really, the indignity of it all is astounding."

I held my tongue. I wanted to point out that she had no

right to complain, being a thief herself. Liam sidled up to me, grim and tight-lipped, and placed a hand on the small of my back.

Yeah, yeah I get it. Don't poke the faery.

"Do you know where they took it?" Caden asked.

"The one who took it lives at the topmost spire."

"Wait, you didn't say *who* took it," Caden said.

Taneisha's grin was wicked. "No, I did not. But you're a clever boy. You'll figure it out. I recommend you hurry, however."

"What's our time frame to complete this round?" I asked.

Taneisha tapped a finger to her lips, as if she was just now considering her answer. "Well, it's not what I'd planned, but it is more tricky. Dangerous even. So, no deadline. Just, don't die, retrieve Caden's seeds, and we'll call it good and get back to our regularly scheduled programming."

That didn't sound ominous. At all. I looked around at the others, who, based on their grim expressions, shared my sentiments.

"So, just to clarify, you've still got all the other items?" Franc asked.

Taneisha held up a hand, her thumb across her palm. "Scout's honor."

Franc cocked his head to the side. "You're a scout?"

Taneisha's eyes widened with surprise. "Well, no. Of course not. But I hear they're quite honorable."

"Someone else's honor is not something you can swear on," Franc said.

"And yet I just did," Taneisha replied with a wink. But then the fae's mercurial nature surfaced again, and her face contorted into a frown as she crossed her arms. "I recommend you leave at once. I even prepared you some travel bags. Each of you get one."

She pointed to an area near the oak door, and then the bags appeared, five in all. I did a quick recount in my head. Yup, only five.

"There's only five," I said.

Taneisha threaded her fingers together in front of her, her expression grave. "Unfortunately, the one lacking honor won't be joining you on Caden's quest."

Of course, all of us looked at Emrys, who at least had the grace not to pretend not to know what she'd accused him of, although he rolled his eyes.

"You can't steal trash," he said.

"Taking a thing not freely given is, definitionally, stealing, Emrys. Even if it is someone's trash."

He planted his hands on his hips, holding his chin high. "So what, I'm just supposed to stay here with you and twiddle my thumbs by the river while the others head out?"

"Nope. That would be tedious." Taneisha raised her right hand and snapped her fingers. In that moment, Emrys disappeared.

I gasped. "What did you do with him?" I asked, feeling proprietary in a way I didn't have a right to be, but there it was.

"Oh, he's fine, just in timeout. He broke the rules, so I've sent him to the penalty box."

"Can you explain the penalty box rules?" Franc asked, his voice strained.

"One, if you break my rules, I'll send you to the penalty box and you'll remain there for one round. Two, there can be only one person in the penalty box. Three, you'll return to the group the following round, assuming no one else breaks the rules and you complete this quest."

"Hypothetically, what happens if someone breaks the rules?" Franc asked.

"The penalty box would reset when I sent the next person into it for their time out," she explained.

"Leaving Emrys... Where?" I asked.

"Nowhere, obviously. Same goes if you don't get Caden's seeds back. Win your quest to free him."

We were deathly quiet for a few seconds. I'd known coming into a fae's dimension gave them power over you. I hadn't truly digested what that meant until now.

"You can't be serious, Taneisha," I pleaded. "Emrys did nothing worth dying over."

Taneisha's face was impassive. "This is not a negotiation. I recommend you get on your way."

"You can't kill him," I said. "You won't."

"I won't kill him," Taneisha replied. "As long as no one else misbehaves, he's fine. Bored, but fine. Truly, when you think about it, it'll be one of you killing him, *if* you break the rules or fail on your quest."

Franc let out a yell, launching himself toward Taneisha, but Caden and Liam blocked him.

"It's not the answer you want," Liam said. "But we can't get out of the game without sacrificing Emrys and our icons. We push on. There's no other option. Well, no other option we're willing to live with."

Franc struggled, even as the words hit home. When he quieted, Liam and Caden let him go. He was the first to grab a bag and walk through the door. One by one, we each followed him.

"Have fun storming the castle!" Taneisha called out after us as we walked through the tree's portal door into our next adventure.

THE END

***

Thank you so much for reading Forbidden Fates! It would mean a lot to me if you could leave a review. A single line or two makes a big difference for other people when deciding if a book is a good fit for them.

The next book in the series, Entangled Essence, is available now.

While Emrys is locked away, the others have no choice but to push forward without him. Can Sera keep the peace between this chosen brotherhood, or will the trials of the mountain crush their hopes and Caden's chance at making peace with his family?

ALSO BY CANDICE BUNDY

The Stolen Legacy Series

***Looted Legacies,* A prequel novella**

Forbidden Fates

Entangled Essence

Hidden Hearts

Reckless Rapture

Sworn Spirits

The Shadow Series

***Shadow in the City,* A prequel novella**

Twinned Shadow

Poisoned Shadow

Shadow Underground

Caught Between Worlds Series

Smoke and Daemons

(previously published as Daemon Whisperer)

Other Works

Ripples, a novella

Open Rack, a contemporary short

WRITING AS CR BUNDY

The Depths of Memory Series

The Dream Sifter

Dreams Manifest

For a list of my full catalog of available titles, visit my candicebundy.com/books page.

ALSO BY PIPER FOX

Academy for Reapers: Paranormal Romance

Big Wolf on Campus Series: Wolf Shifter Football Romances

The Stolen Legacy Series: Paranormal Reverse Harem

Midnight Huntress Series: Paranormal Reverse Harem

Alien Warriors of New Dilaria Series: Sci-Fi Reverse Harem

The Ironhaven Pack Series: Wolf Shifter Romances

The Dragon Space Order Bride Series: Sci-Fi Romance

ALSO BY PIPER FOX

[Bears of Crooked Creek](): A Bear Shifter Romance Series

[Seven Brides For Seven Demons](): A Demon Romance Series

[Last Warriors of Dilaria](): A Sci-Fi Romance Series

The Immortal Blood Series: Vampire Romance

About Candice Bundy

Candice lives in Denver, Colorado with her son and their cat Newt. A professional hedonist, rabble-rouser, winemaker, and goat-herder, she adores archeology and mythology. Candice focuses on habit hacking to meet minimalist, health, productivity, and positive mojo goals, and sometimes even blogs about it. An unrepentant epicurean, she grows heirloom tomatoes and ferments a variety of sauerkraut, sourdough, kombucha, pickles, and water kefir.

If you would like to know when she has new books out, please sign up for her newsletter here. Email her if the mood strikes you.

For more information:
candicebundy.com
candice@candicebundy.com

ABOUT PIPER FOX

Piper Fox writes steamy paranormal romances for sassy, strong-willed women and the sexy, alpha men who love them.

Follow her on:
Facebook: facebook.com/PiperFoxAuthor
Bookbub: https://www.bookbub.com/profile/piper-fox

Made in the USA
Middletown, DE
07 January 2024